I
Am
the
Universe

BARBARA
CORCORAN

 Harcourt Brace Jovanovich, Inc.
Orlando   Austin   San Diego   Chicago   Dallas   New York

As a part of the HBJ TREASURY OF LITERATURE, 1993 Edition, this
edition is published by special arrangement with Atheneum Publishers, an imprint
of Macmillan Publishing Company.

Grateful acknowledgment is made to Atheneum Publishers, an imprint of
Macmillan Publishing Company for permission to reprint I Am the Universe
by Barbara Corcoran. Copyright © 1986 by Barbara Corcoran.

Cover painting copyright © 1986 by Judith Gwyn Brown.

Printed in the United States of America

ISBN 0-15-300366-9

3 4 5 6 7 8 9 10   059   96   95   94   93

TO
Patty,
with love
&
thanks

I
Am
the
Universe

Chapter One

TODAY MRS. RAMER assigned us a paper on who we are. That's all I need, having to figure out who I am! Here we are in the last semester of the eighth grade, psyching ourselves up for the switch in the fall from this ugly old familiar building where I've been since the first grade, to that enormous alien-looking bunch of buildings on the south side of town, and I have to stop and figure out who I am?

Besides, if I'm going to be sure even of a C in math, I have to concentrate on that for the rest of the year. I've got a safe B in my other subjects and an A in English, but for math I have to slave.

"It's that psychotherapist she's been going to," my friend Anna said. She was talking about Mrs. Ramer. "She's into identity and all that." Nobody but Anna would have found out that Mrs. Ramer was in therapy.

It was true, though. One Saturday morning we'd hung around the mental health clinic, and we'd seen her come out. I'd be in therapy too if I had to teach us.

"So can you write a paper about who you are?" I said to Anna. "I mean do you *know*?"

"No sweat," Anna said.

I guess everybody but me knows who they are. Nobody else in the class seemed to be upset by the assignment. Personally I thought it was diabolical.

Besides, I had other things to worry about. Like my mother's headaches. She says they're just tiresome old migraines, but she never had them before. And they are so bad, it makes my own head hurt to see her. What if they mean something awful? Can you get cancer of the head? Daddy says I'm a worrier; but I try not to be, especially since the other kids pick up on it, Daniel most of all.

Daniel is my eight-year-old brother. He's the oddball in the family. I keep feeling that he's very bright, but then he's almost flunking third grade, so I could be wrong. My brother Andrew is fourteen. He plays the guitar, and he's saving up for a hammered dulcimer. Terry is our little sister. She's in nursery school. Okay, so that's who everybody else is, but who am I?

I'll be thirteen in July. I like to write stories. I hate math, and I'm clumsy at PE. When I look in the mirror, I get depressed. The rest of my family range from good-looking to beautiful, but I look like nothing. It makes me feel as if I have no control over my life.

4

I heard Aunt Meg talking about me to Mom once, and she said, "What a shame that Kit is so plain."

Mom got mad, which meant she knew Aunt Meg was right but she wasn't about to admit it. She said, "Kit is just fine. She has that gorgeous hair, dark gold and ripply—"

"—and tied up tight in braids," Aunt Meg said.

"She has excellent bones. She's going to be a very attractive woman."

Aunt Meg laughed and changed the subject. It's a family joke how Mom defends her children. I appreciate it, but I wish she wouldn't do it. Aunt Meg is right, I'm plain. My eyes are all right, I guess, dark blue like Daniel's, only he has those long lashes. But Daddy won't let me get my hair cut, so I have these childish braids, and my mouth is solid braces. I have Daddy's nose—a beak, really, and freckled. If you're going to have freckles, you ought to have a cute little pug nose like Daniel's. Oh, well. Vanity, vanity, all is vanity, saith the preacher.

I left Anna and went down to the third grade end of the building to see if Daniel wanted to walk home with me. Sometimes he does, sometimes he doesn't. You never know about Daniel.

Kids were barreling past me and talking at the top of their lungs. We're outside the city limits, so we still have the old first-through-eighth-grades-all-in-one-building system, instead of the new city system of separate elementary and middle schools. So this old ramshackle place is wall-to-wall kids, all shrieking. I thought of Mrs. Ramer and her therapist.

Everybody had left the third grade room except Daniel and Mr. Hergesheimer, so I leaned against the wall to wait. It was not an unusual situation. Daniel never makes any trouble in school, but he drives his teachers crazy because he never does the work. My parents have scolded and threatened and punished and offered rewards, but nothing has done the trick. He daydreams.

I heard Mr. Hergesheimer raise his voice. I glanced in. The two of them were standing in front of the desk. Mr. Hergesheimer's hair was standing straight up as if he'd just had an electric shock, but that's not unusual. He's a good teacher—I had him myself in the third grade—but he's not famous for his patience.

Daniel was peering at Mr. Hergesheimer over the top of his glasses. They slide down his nose all the time. Mom says it makes him look like a little owl.

"You," Mr. Hergesheimer was saying, "could be my best student." He was getting pink in the face. "A-one. Instead what do you do? Nothing. N-o-t-h-i-n-g. No papers, no homework, no answers in class. And you're quite likely to flunk the third grade, do you realize that? You, Daniel Esterly, with an IQ of a hundred and forty. It's outrageous."

Daniel looked interested. "Is a hundred and forty a good IQ?"

"It's practically genius," Mr. Hergesheimer

roared. Then he looked uncomfortable. "You're not supposed to know your scores. Darn you, Daniel, you annoyed it out of me."

"Genius?" Daniel said thoughtfully. "No kidding?"

"Oh, go home, Daniel. You elevate my blood pressure." Mr. Hergesheimer whirled around and got tangled in the big paper Mobius curve that he had hung up to show the class how Einstein thought the universe was shaped.

Daniel came out into the corridor. His buddy Tony came whooping along.

"Hey, Dan, want to play Stuffed Animal Killers?"

"No," Daniel said.

Daniel invented Stuffed Animal Killers several years ago. He and Tony used yardsticks for swords and pillow cases to foil the force field of the enemy, and they would dash and thrash all over the backyard. But Daniel had grown tired of the game and Tony hadn't. Tony was always a couple of beats behind Daniel.

"I'm going to walk home backwards," Daniel said.

"Why? You'll stub your toe," Tony said.

"Heel."

"Huh?"

"You can't stub your toe walking backwards."

"Yeah?" Tony gave him a blank stare. Tony is not the brightest kid in town. He watched as Daniel walked backwards down the school steps. "He's nuts," he muttered, and ran off.

I watched Daniel negotiate the school grounds, ignoring kids who asked him what he was doing. There was no use asking him why he did the things he did. I don't think he knew himself, sometimes. When he was little, he used to put his clothes on backwards and even inside out. Mom never knew for sure if he didn't know any better or just wanted to be different. Sometimes she says to him, "Why can't you be more like Kit? She always has a reason for what she does." Well, I *give* a reason, but it's not always the right one. My parents respect reasons, so I pretend to be more "sensible" than I really am. Nobody besides me knows all the stuff that goes on in my head.

I got my bike and rode home. I passed Daniel as he was crossing an intersection. He made it all right. A woman with a baby in a stroller said, "Mind the curb, honey."

I was thinking about Mom as I rode into our street. I'd been thinking about her all day. Usually she would be in the kitchen correcting freshman themes. She taught part time at the university. I crossed my fingers while I put my bike in the garage. Make her be there. But she wasn't. Only Andrew was there, drinking milk.

"Where's Mom?" I was scared to hear the answer.

"Lying down." He wiped his mouth with the back of his hand. He's going through a stage where his manners are atrocious. But he's so good-looking and so popular, he can get away with almost anything.

8

"Has she got a headache?" My voice sounded funny.

"Yeah. Dad said for us to be quiet. Keep an eye on Terry when she wakes up, will you?"

Our father teaches history of the ancient world at the university.

I sat down and looked at the freshman themes. She had corrected three of them. She says I write better than most of her students. But it's because that's what I'm going to be: a writer.

"My Summer With the Mountain Goats" was the title of the one on top. He had made a mistake in the very first sentence. An adverb where there should have been an adjective. Mom had scribbled ADJ in red ink. I could tell by her writing that she was exasperated.

"Did she take her pills?" I asked Andrew. It made my own head ache to think of her pain.

He looked at me. "Yeah, I guess. Hey, don't worry, Kit. It's just a headache." Andrew will never worry about anything till it grabs him by the throat and wrestles him to the ground.

Daniel came into the kitchen still walking backwards.

"What are you walking backwards for?" Andrew asked him.

"To see where I've been." Daniel began to make his favorite sandwich. When Mom isn't there to restrain him, he uses a layer of peanut butter, then strawberry jam, two slices of tomato, a piece of liverwurst, and a great slather of mayonnaise. It's enough to make you lose your appetite forever.

Andrew shuddered and left the room.

It was naptime for Terry. The house was quiet. I wondered if Mrs. Hume would come to cook dinner. She's a neighbor, and sometimes she helps us out when Mom is sick. She makes peculiar meals: the last time it was frozen tamales and boiled potatoes and raw green peppers. Daddy hates Mexican food, but of course he didn't say so to Mrs. Hume. I can't stand raw peppers. The potatoes were boiled too long and were mushy. But Daddy says we should be thankful for Mrs. Hume's kindness. I guess I am, but I'd rather fix dinner myself.

Daniel's cat, Mister Quickly, came into the room and leaped onto Daniel's shoulder. He's a handsome cat, silvery gray with almost invisible black stripes going around him. He has green eyes, and you can see him thinking. He puts up with the rest of us, but he is definitely Daniel's cat.

"Have I got news for you," Daniel said to Mister Q.

I wondered if Daniel would tell us what Mr. Hergesheimer said about his IQ. If it were me, I'd keep it a secret so I wouldn't have to live up to it all the time. So maybe that's part of who I am: cowardly.

Mom had folded back the local paper to the page where the weekly column of kids' literary efforts were. I had a poem there, just a quatrain, no big deal. Next to it there was a second grader's poem that said, "Here lies Jack Magone, looked at truth and turned to stone." I thought that was neat for a second grader. Our schools make a big effort to get everybody to write. I used to like getting in the column, but now I feel stupid. I'm too old. Well, after this year, no more. Maybe I'll get something in the high school paper . . . ha ha, fat chance.

I went upstairs. Mom was lying on her back with her eyes closed and a washcloth on her head. I wondered if I should ask her if she'd like it made colder, but she might be asleep. I didn't know what to do. I hate it when I don't know what to do.

She opened her eyes a little slit and gave me a shadow of a smile. "Hello, sweetie." Her voice was small.

"I'm sorry your head hurts. Do you want me to cool off the washcloth?"

"No, thanks, dear. I took my pills. They're helping." She moved her hand kind of weakly, and the washcloth fell onto her pillow. I picked it up so it wouldn't make her pillow all wet. She closed her eyes again. That dreamy little smile stayed on her face. I wondered if the pills were habit-forming. What if she got addicted?

Chapter

Two

I COULD HEAR TERRY getting up from her nap. If I didn't stop her, she'd make a racket and wake Mom. She's always all over the place when she wakes up. Daddy calls her the Dynamo.

So I lured her into my room. Terry doesn't look at all like me. She's small and dark and *piquant*. I looked that word up the other day, and that's Terry all right.

"You have to be quiet. Mom's got a headache."

She stuck out her lower lip. "I want to tell Mommy what I dreamed."

"Later. You can tell me if you want to."

She didn't want to. She probably didn't even have a dream. She likes attention. And gets it.

Daniel came along the hall. He had tied a new red ribbon around Lamb's neck. He doesn't play with

Lamb much any more, but he used to take him every-where, even to church, and Lamb would pray quite loudly in a bleating kind of voice. Andrew thought it was terrible, but Daddy said Lamb had as much right to pray as anybody.

"I'm going to let Mom have Lamb," Daniel said. "For the afternoon. She doesn't feel good."

"Later, Daniel, okay? She's asleep."

He looked disappointed, but Daniel is not one to argue. "I'm going to the park to see Uncle Walt," he said.

It was an idea. A way to get noisy Terry out of the house. "We'll come with you."

He made a face.

"We won't bother you. I want the house to be quiet for Mom."

He sighed. "All right. I'm going in five minutes."

"I want to go to the park with Daniel," Terry said.

"You're going to. Put on your shoes."

Uncle Walt isn't really our uncle. He's a friend. We met him when Daddy ran into him. Daddy is a terrible driver, and he smashed right into Uncle Walt in a crosswalk and broke his leg. We kept him at our house till he was better, and we all got very fond of him. He lives on Social Security and his Air Force pension in a tiny room over the hardware store. He has had a very interesting life, and he's traveled all over, besides being in two wars. He plays the harmonica.

Daniel was ready. As usual, he had filled up his

bookbag as if he were going around the world. Just to go to the park he was taking *The Knights of the Round Table,* his radio, a chocolate almond bar for Uncle Walt, big size, a clean T-shirt, his toothbrush, and four bananas. He said you never could tell what would happen. "Somebody might drop a bomb, and we'd have to live in a cave for a year."

I reminded him about homework, but he just shook his head. He really may get kept back in the third grade. Having a high IQ isn't much good if you don't use it.

When I settled Terry on the handlebars of my bike, Daniel and Mister Q were already zooming down the street on Dan's bike. He and Q often go on long rides alone, and he takes care of that bike as if it were a Jaguar or something.

I went slowly because Terry squirms, so when we got to the bicycle parking lot, Daniel was already disappearing across the narrow wooden bridge that goes over the river. I followed with Terry, who always yips and squeals a lot when she looks down into the river. I don't think she's really scared; she just likes to get attention.

I let her go on ahead after Daniel, up the trail, but I slowed down because I wanted to check on the trillium. I was always afraid somebody would have found it and picked it. It grows high on the bank, and you probably wouldn't notice it if you weren't looking for it.

It was a warm day, the first of May, and already the snowy white petals were taking on a pinkish look. I was trying to think of a poem about them. Trillium isn't an easy word to rhyme.

A jogger ran by me. He came along so silently, he startled me. But he just said, "Nice day," and kept on going.

The north part of the park is the start of a wilderness area: it's quite steep, with woods on one side and on the other side a slopey cliff that goes down to the river. The spring rains had filled the river almost to flood stage, and it looked wonderful churning along fast and white.

Mom says trillium is sometimes called Western Wake-a-Robin. Maybe I could call it that in the poem. Wake-a-Robin, Wake-a-Robin, wake to my call . . . No, no good.

I climbed the hill and pretty soon I came to the wooden bench where Uncle Walt always sits. He runs up here from the park entrance, almost a mile away. He doesn't jog, he runs. Pretty good for a man his age with a gimpy leg. He doesn't look old at all. He just has a little gray in his thick hair, and he's muscular. He's been in China and Tibet among other places.

Terry was climbing into his lap, and Daniel was methodically unpacking his shoulder bag, all except the shirt and toothbrush. He gave Uncle Walt the Hershey bar.

"Thanks," Uncle Walt said in his deep voice. "That'll be real tasty. And if I can get Saint Teresa here out of my hair, I'll share it. Good afternoon, Katharine."

"Good afternoon," I said. I sat down with my back to a pine tree to read *Tiger Eyes*. "Terry, leave Uncle Walt alone."

She wrapped her arms around his neck.

"Or you won't get any chocolate," Daniel said.

I knew he wished we hadn't come. He and Uncle Walt have long private talks. They really like each other.

As Uncle Walt began to divide the candy bar, Daniel said, "You don't have to share it. It's for you."

"Share and share alike," Uncle Walt said. He gave a piece to Terry and set her on the ground. She stuffed her face with chocolate.

Uncle Walt gave some to me and to Daniel, who fed a bite to Mister Q. That cat has very odd tastes. His favorite food of all is Doritos. On Friday nights Daniel and Mr. Q curl up on Daniel's bed with a bag of Doritos and listen to "Mystery Theater of the Air."

Uncle Walt sat with his left leg out in front of him. It aches where it was broken by Daddy's car. I don't know how he runs on it, but he does.

Daniel said, "Is your leg hurting today?"

"Just a smidgen," he said. "Just an iota."

"I'm surprised you don't sue Daddy," Daniel said.

"Now why would I do an unfriendly thing like that? You were all real good to me after the accident."

"Justice is justice," Daniel said, looking severe.

"And good will is good will. Your daddy is a kindly man. He just happens to be a bad driver."

"Mama says he ought not to be allowed on the road," Terry said, with her mouth full.

"Terry," I said. You'd think they'd both know enough not to bad-mouth their parents in public.

Mister Q leaped off Daniel's lap and chased a squirrel up a tree. The squirrel ran out on a limb that swayed as if it would dump him off. Mister Q looked at him a minute and then came back down the tree.

"That is a cautious cat," Uncle Walt said. "A sensible cat. A lesson to us all."

Daniel gathered his cat into his arms. "I have news for you." He let half a minute go by, and then he said, "I have a hundred forty IQ. That's almost genius."

Mister Q gently bit Daniel's ear.

"Well, well," Uncle Walt said. "Congratulations. What are you going to do with your genius?"

Daniel thought about it. "I don't think I have to do anything with it. It just *is*."

"I don't believe anything just is. Everything is in motion. You remember how we talked about the electrons and the protons and all that, whirling around and around. And the quarks. Don't forget the quarks. All of 'em spinning and zipping all over the universe. Heed the words of James Joyce: 'Three quarks for Muster Mark! Sure he hasn't got much of a bark, And sure any he has it's all beside the mark.' "

"I don't know what that means," Daniel said.

"Neither do I, but it has a nice ring to it," Uncle Walt said.

I said, "Did James Joyce really say that?"

"Yes, ma'am, in *Finnegan's Wake*, a very interesting book that I do not understand a word of."

I've never read Joyce. I decided I would, to see if I could understand it.

Daniel handed around the bananas.

"This morning on 'Star Date,' " Uncle Walt said, peeling his banana neatly, "it was said that some scientists believe people are the universe looking at itself."

Daniel stopped halfway to taking a bite out of his banana. "I like that."

"Figured you would," Uncle Walt said. He folded his banana peel and buried it in a little hole that he dug with the heel of his boot. Mister Q came and dug it up. "That cat has too much intellectual curiosity." Uncle Walt buried the peel again and shooed Mister Q away. He is a very neat man. He took his harmonica out of his pocket.

"Oh, goodie," Terry said, her mouth full of banana. "Play." (Never mind "please.")

Uncle Walt played long ago with Pete Seeger, and he learned a lot from Peter Cotton, who Uncle Walt says is the greatest harmonica player of all. He started off with "Freight Train," which I like very much. Then he played "Down by the Riverside," and then he began to play his own music, which is different. Sometimes it's haunting and sad, sometimes joyful, tunes you want to dance to.

The music took me right away from where we were. First it was Spain, where Uncle Walt fought in the Civil War and got a bullet through his shoulder. Then I was flying in his P-38 in World War II, only we weren't shooting anyone. But often it was another world that no one but Uncle Walt and I could see. Some of it was like the pictures in Mom's copy of *The Book of Kells*, odd-looking little monks with pointed hats, and angels in vivid colors and lots of gold all over. And then the music was wild and sweet, and I wanted to dance and cry all at once.

Daniel had his eyes closed. Once when I asked him what he saw when Uncle Walt played, he said, "I see my enclosed garden and the cloister where I live." He has dreamed all his life about a walled-in garden and a cloister.

Even Terry kept quiet while Uncle Walt played. When he stopped, we all sat still for a few minutes. Then Terry jumped on Uncle Walt again and said, as if it was wonderful news, "Our mama is sick. She might die."

It seemed to me the words boomed across the river and echoed back. And my ears rang the way they do when you have a fever.

Daniel jumped up, spilling Mister Q. He swung his arm out and hit Terry on the shoulder. "That's a lie!" His voice sounded choked.

Terry looked surprised, and then she began to wail.

"She didn't mean it," I said to Daniel.

"She shouldn't tell such terrible lies."

My chest felt tight. Suddenly I had to make sure Mom was all right. "Let's go home. Mom might want you to sing to her." I lifted the sobbing Terry out of Uncle Walt's lap. "Thanks for playing for us."

He nodded, looking sad, and that made me angry. If grownups were going to look sad about my mother, that meant they thought something terrible was going to happen. And that couldn't be true. People get headaches every day, don't they?

I put Terry down, grabbed her hand and ran down the hill. She bounced and tripped and yelled, but I didn't stop.

Chapter
Three

MRS. HUME was putting frozen egg foo yong in the oven. She's great for ethnic foods. "There you are, honey," she said in her loud cheerful voice. "I was just leaving. The egg foo yong will be ready in about twenty minutes. No, make it thirty. Well, you can check. I washed some carrots for your Vitamin A. And I opened a can of peas. There's a Sara Lee chocolate cake defrosting."

"Thanks very much, Mrs. Hume. We really appreciate it." And really we did. But Andrew is allergic to eggs, and if you ever tried to eat raw carrots with braces on your teeth, you understand my problem. The cake looked good though.

I could hear the sound of Andrew's guitar from the basement room he's made into a studio. I wondered why Mrs. Hume hadn't told *him* to watch the egg foo yong. Because he's a boy, that's why. She's one of those people who think getting dinner on the table is woman's work. We don't go for that stuff in our family. We all do whatever needs to be done.

Then I realized I shouldn't resent Mrs. Hume. She was only trying to do her Christian duty.

Daniel came in and looked in the oven. "Omelet?" He was wearing his battered old cowboy hat.

"Egg foo yong."

"Looks like omelet to me. Andrew won't eat it." He looked at me over his glasses. "Mom feels better, only a little pale. I'm going to sing her cowboy songs after dinner."

"That's nice." Everybody in this family is musical but me and Daddy. He says we have a tin ear, but I love music so my ear can't be all tinny.

Daddy's car drove into the yard, and Daniel ran out to meet him. I began to set the table. Mrs. Hume had put the bread knife in with the dress-up silver, and it took me a while to find it. Daddy is fussy about bread. He wants it fresh and unsliced, preferably whole wheat or gluten or else white with sesame seeds. Sesame seeds are good, but they stick in my braces.

I could hear Terry upstairs bothering Mom, but then she heard Daddy and came galloping down. She threw herself at him as he came in the door. My father is very big, both sideways and up and down. He wanted to play football in college, but the coach turned him down because he always dropped the ball. He still drops things. He says he has poorly developed small motor skills. Mom says he's clumsy.

He has this thick black beard that he sort of hides behind when he's somewhere he doesn't want to be. He's beginning to get a little bit bald on top. He made the kitchen shrink as he walked in, gave me a hug and said, "How's your mother?"

"I told you," Daniel said. "You don't listen."

Daddy looked down at him with the crooked grin that shows his chipped tooth in front. "I listened, Dan. You said her headache was gone and she's feeling pale. I always like to get a second opinion."

"She feels better," I said.

"Good." He looked relieved. He and my mom really like each other. "How was your day?"

"We went to the park," Terry babbled. "I sat in Uncle Walt's lap and he played the 'monica."

"*Har*-monica," Daniel said.

"How is Walt?" Daddy was inching toward the door. You could tell he was dying to go see Mom, but he didn't want to be rude to his children.

"His leg hurts," Daniel said. "I told him he ought to sue you."

Daddy made a face. "Thanks a million, son." He put Terry down and escaped upstairs.

When I went down to the basement to call Andrew for dinner, he was listening to a tape. He had that rapt look he gets when it's music he likes. He waved at me to wait for the tape to end. It was a woman singing, "That's No Way for Me to Get Along." She was playing a nice tricky guitar accompaniment. Andrew had taught me to listen for good breaks.

When it was finished, he said, "Wow! Isn't she great? I read about her in *Rolling Stone*. Queen of the Delta Blues. She plays a nifty guitar."

"And sings good."

"Right." But he was always more interested in the guitar.

"Dinner's ready."

"Be right there."

He'd fixed up the room really neat. Sometimes he slept down there on the old couch that was in Daddy's office until the stuffing began to fall out. For equipment he had a turntable and two tape decks, one he got for Christmas and one he swapped with another kid for a radio he didn't want, a good AM-FM radio that Aunt Meg gave him, and amplifiers and mikes. It looked like a real recording studio. On the wall there were posters of The Grateful Dead and of Rod Stewart, an old poster of Joan Baez that Mom had saved for years, and a framed picture of Pete and Mike Seeger that Uncle Walt gave him. It was signed, "To our good friend Walt, from Mike and Pete."

I remembered the egg foo yong and flew back upstairs to check on it. It looked done. I called Daddy and the kids and got things on the table. Andrew helped. When he saw the foo yong, he gagged. "I can't eat that."

"I know. You want me to make you a sandwich?"

"I'll make it. There's roast beef left."

The egg foo yong turned out to be still frozen in the middle, so we all had roast beef sandwiches. The cake was good, except for the slivers of ice.

"Tomorrow night," Daddy said, "we'll go out to dinner."

"Goody," Terry said. "Big Macs." She always said that, although we seldom went to McDonald's. Daddy said it was plastic.

"Is Mama eating that foo yong crap?" Daniel said.

"Daniel," Daddy said. "That's no way to talk. Did anyone remember to thank Mrs. Hume?"

"I did," I said.

"She made your mother some nice chicken soup and toast and tea."

"Made soup out of a can," Daniel said.

"Daniel! That's enough!"

Daniel knew enough to change the subject. "Mom is feeling better, isn't she."

"Yes, she is."

"Why don't we go to the Sheraton tomorrow night?" Andrew said.

"If I get my paycheck," Daddy said.

I knew he was feeling good because Mom was better. Me, too. I wondered why we all got so upset up in the park.

"My milk's got a bug in it," Terry said.

"Terry, you're gross," Andrew said.

"I can't drink it."

Daniel looked at it. "It has not."

"It has too. I can't drink it."

"You know you could if you just would," Daniel said.

Andrew looked thoughtful. "You know you could if you only would . . . That sounds like a song."

"Hey, I just wrote a song," Daniel said.

"You only wrote the title, Squirt." He got up from the table humming a tune to fit the words. "Dan, will you take my turn to do the dishes? I've got a date."

"We're not through this meal, Andrew," Daddy said.

"But Dad . . ."

"Sit down."

This was fairly new, Andrew having dates. We hadn't gotten used to it. It seemed to be a whole bunch of different girls. I didn't think much of the ones I'd seen. Blonde and giggly. I could write a theme about people I *don't* want to be.

"I have an announcement to make," Daniel said. He rang his knife against his glass for attention.

"Quickly then," Daddy said. "Andrew has a date." Sometimes he swaps sides so fast you can't keep up with him.

Daniel stood up and looked at each one of us. "I am the universe." He sat down and waited.

No one said anything for a minute. I mean what can you say to a statement like that?

Then Daddy said vaguely, "How nice for you."

"That child," Andrew said, "needs a shrink."

Terry said in a fast little song, "I am the sun and the moon and the stars and that's better than any old universe."

"I think we can all be excused now," Daddy said.

I helped Daniel wash the dishes. He was quiet. Later he went upstairs and sang cowboy songs to Mom. When I got him to bed, he snuggled down with Lamb and said, "I knew Terry was a liar. Mama just had a headache, and she's all better. She liked my songs."

I kissed the top of his head. I don't usually do that kind of thing, but he looked so little, with Lamb's head beside his on the pillow. "Good night, O Universe."

He stared at me for a second, with those huge dark blue eyes. Then he giggled.

Later in bed I thought how he said he was the universe as if it seemed perfectly natural to him. Even my eight-year-old brother knows who he is; and me, I haven't a clue. Maybe there are people who are nobody, and I am one of them.

Chapter

Four

I THOUGHT a lot about Mrs. Ramer's assignment. I wanted to keep up my record of A's on my themes, but also I felt uneasy about finding it so hard to say who I was.

I looked at some of Daddy's books, especially *Great Ages of Western Philosophy*. I didn't get very far. Somebody named Descartes said, "I think, therefore I am." But therefore I am what? Ralph Waldo Emerson seemed to think he was a tree. In my opinion philosophy is an invention intended to confuse people into total panic. The more I thought about it, the more depressed I got.

I hoped and prayed that Mrs. Ramer wouldn't ask me to read my paper. I had poured my feelings into it, and it's my experience that the more you unload your heart and soul on paper, the more likely people are not to get it.

She called on me.

"Whoever I Am," by Katharine Esterly.

"One who embarks on a voyage of self-discovery sets forth in very stormy seas. First of all he runs into the reefs and shoals labeled 'Things I am Not.' Here are some of the sharp obstructions this writer smashed into.

"One: I am not an adult."

(This got the first burst of laughter from the class, and I knew right then they were going to laugh at every single emotion I had anguished through.)

"Two: I am not a child.

"Therefore, what am I? I am an eighth grader, aged twelve, which is precisely nothing. I am a neither nor."

(Applause. Laughter.)

"In July I will be a teenager, but since no one has adequately defined that term, I do not look forward to that condition with any hope.

"Three: I am not a writer. Yet. I can only cross my fingers and pray. As somebody said, 'There's many a slip twixt the pen and the check.' "

(This time I expected a laugh and didn't get it.)

"So what am I? Well, I am a pair of hands when my mother wants the dishes washed. Soapy hands. I am a pair of ears when my brother wants me to tell him how great his music is. I am a pair of arms when my little sister wakes up from a bad dream and wants to be held. I am two feet when my mother wants something at the store. I am a mind when Mr. Blankenship wants the science experiment finished. I am two ears when my father wants to tell his funny story about the ancient Phoenicians one more time.

"I could go on listing what I am and am not, but the point is made. I am a series of other people's needs. As I went on with my voyage, I found myself in heavy surf. I bounced and dropped and bounced up again. If you do this very long, you can get quite seasick."

(Much laughter.)

"Out in those heavy seas I found nothing. I had to conclude that there is no such thing as me."

I SAT DOWN, feeling sick. Not seasick but landsick, heartsick, soulsick. They were laughing and applauding as if I were Eddie Murphy or The Three Stooges. I had peeled away the layers of what I'd always assumed was myself, and I found nothing there. I wanted to burst into tears.

Mrs. Ramer was smiling broadly. "Comments, people?" She always says that.

Dennis Rourke raised his hand. "She's got four ears," he said, and the class practically fell on the floor laughing. They sounded like twenty-seven donkeys braying.

I knew I'd put in ears twice, but I couldn't change it without leaving out Andrew or Daddy.

"She's a comedian, that's who she is," Mary Borovich said. She meant it as a compliment.

To my classmates, I am a pair of feeble jokes.

It is no joke to me. I can't get it off my mind. I am nobody.

Chapter Five

THIS WAS A DAY fraught with emotion, and I do mean fraught. When I got home from school, I was feeling very excited. It was possible I was going to establish a me, Katharine Esterly, after all. Katharine Esterly, author.

The house smelled like Thanksgiving in May. Mom was cooking a turkey. Our house is a huge Victorian heap set up against a mountain at the end of a dead-end street. In winter it is dark and cold, but in spring the sun turns it into an enchanted castle, with trees all around it making green and yellow clouds. Mom's Aunt Geraldine gave her the house. Aunt Geraldine was the famous one in the family. Ten years in the state legislature, four in Washington, D.C., as a lobbyist for the lumber industry. Mom was her secretary before she got married. Daddy makes fun of Aunt Geraldine, and Mom gets mad. "You pioneer women of the West," he says. He's from Pennsylvania.

Mom was making stuffing and reading a theme at the same time. She is the only person I know who looks wonderful in glasses. Her hair is dark gold, and she wears it in a knot at the back of her head. She has brown eyes with gold flecks in them, and she's almost as tall as Daddy.

"I've got news," I said.

She leaned over the pile of chopped onions and roasted chestnuts and the freshman theme that was paper-clipped to the rack that's supposed to hold cookbooks, and she kissed me on the nose. "It looks like good news. Tell me."

The little kitchen radio was playing "Send in the Clowns," and I knew she was listening to that too, because it's her favorite popular song. She dumped the onions and chopped chestnuts into a bowl. "What is it, sweetie?"

Daniel came into the kitchen and began to make himself a sandwich.

"Kit has news," Mom said.

He looked at me with his intent, inquisitive look. I heard Terry upstairs, getting up from her nap and singing "The Farmer in the Dell." I knew I'd better hurry, or Mom wouldn't be able to listen.

"Well, there's a writer coming for a week. A real writer that's been published." I speeded up as I heard

Terry start downstairs. "We're having a contest. The one that writes the best story gets to spend time with her. Alone. Like a one-on-one workshop. She'll teach us how to get published."

"That's wonderful," Mom said. I could see she really was pleased. "Have you got an idea for a story?"

"Give her 'The Garter Snake Named Phoebe Who Was Afraid of Little Girls,'" Daniel said.

"Oh, Dan. I wrote that in the sixth grade." Actually I had made it up first one night when I was trying to keep him from thinking about how miserable he felt with the flu. It was a silly story. At Girl Scout Camp our nature counselor had had us hold a little garter snake, so we wouldn't be afraid of it, and I got to thinking about the snake getting dropped on its head and getting a trauma about little girls.

"It's your best story," Daniel said.

Mom laughed. "That's like telling Shakespeare that *Love's Labour Lost* is his finest play."

"I don't get it," Daniel said.

"It was his first one. Daniel, don't put so much mayonnaise on your sandwich. It's not good for you. Why don't you sprinkle some sprouts on top?"

"Yuk," Daniel said.

Andrew came in, slamming the door. He looked excited. "Mom, I asked Bonnie to dinner."

Mom frowned. "Andrew! You could at least have consulted me."

"I did it on the spur of the moment. You said our friends were always welcome."

"Well, they are, but I like to know about it."

"Mom, you do know. I'm telling you."

She looked exasperated. "Next time tell me in advance. Or better still, don't *tell* me, *ask* me."

"Who's Bonnie?" I asked him. I couldn't remember a girl by that name.

"She's in third year high school," Andrew said, trying not to look proud. Andrew is only a freshman.

"Well," Mom said, "you can wash the celery, Andrew. And please remove the strings this time."

Mister Q was curled around Daniel's feet, looking as contented as if he and Daniel had the kitchen to themselves. He was reading one of the Narnia books—Daniel, I mean, not Mister Q. Daniel is always reading one of the Narnia books, over and over.

Terry burst into the room singing "The Farmer in the Dell" at the top of her lungs.

Mom rolled her eyes. I thought, no wonder she gets headaches. "What do you want me to do?" I asked her.

"Honey, would you mind polishing the silver? I wasn't going to do it today, but if we're having company . . . Terry, not so loud, dear."

It was that kind of afternoon. I didn't care, though, because I was so happy Mom was still feeling good, and besides, I had the Visiting Author to think about. I had it in my mind to do a story about a Chinese girl, my age, who lived here in the nineteenth century. A lot of Chinese men worked on the railroad when it was first built through to the west. They worked very hard under terrible conditions for practically no pay. There was a Chinese cemetery behind the old River School, which isn't used any more. When they built the school, they made a park behind it that runs down to the river. I don't know whether they dug up the Chinese bones or just covered them up. There's a plaque among the trees that says this was the Chinese cemetery.

I guess there weren't any women with them, but I could invent a woman that this girl's father met some-where along the way. It would be a very hard thing for this Chinese girl to live in our town in those days. She would be awfully lonesome.

I realized I was polishing the same tablespoon over and over, trying to decide what would happen to my Chinese girl. Andrew was in our big old living room polishing Mom's antique furniture. Daniel and Mister Q were vacuuming the rugs. Mister Q hates the vacuum cleaner, and he had wrapped himself around Daniel's neck as if his life were in danger. Terry was sitting on the floor right in Mom's way, eating a piece of celery and talking to her Raggedy Ann. Mom was putting a chocolate meringue pie in the oven. I wonder some-times what it would be like to be an only child. I don't think I'd like it.

Late that afternoon Andrew spent forty-five minutes in the bathroom. He even shaved, although he has practically nothing to shave off except a few dark hairs on his upper lip. When he was ready to go and get this Bonnie person in Dad's car, he looked like an illustration from the Brooks Brothers catalog that Daddy gets although he never orders anything.

Mom looked at him, and then she sighed. "He's growing up," she said to nobody in particular.

"He doesn't have a grown-up driver's license," Daniel said. "He's not supposed to drive without an adult."

She shook her head. "I know. But your father let him this one time. Bonnie lives only three blocks away."

"Is there something wrong with her legs?" Daniel said.

"Whose legs?" Terry said.

We were in the living room, and Mom was arranging a bowl of potato chips and another bowl of the dip she makes with cream cheese and clam juice. There were pretzels, too. Daddy came down from his study.

"It looks as if the Queen of England is coming," he said.

"Queen who?" Terry said. She was making Raggedy Ann tap dance.

"Daniel, dear," Mom said, "go wash up and put on a clean shirt, please."

"She isn't coming to see me," Daniel said.

3 7

"Daniel . . ." Mom was beginning to look a little tired.

"As soon as I finish this chapter."

"Daniel!" Daddy said.

"Yes sir." Daniel got up, looking pained, and went upstairs muttering.

"We have to put the cat out," Mom said. "This girl is allergic to cats."

That made me mad. "Why do we have to rearrange our whole lives—" I began. But Mom gave me a look, and I stopped.

"We'll go through it again when you bring your first date home," Daddy said.

"Never," I said. "I'm not going to have dates."

"Ho-ho," he said. "Shall we have a small fire in the fireplace?" he asked Mom. "The evenings are still cool."

"That would be nice, dear."

I was disgusted with the way the whole family was acting; it was as if we really were going to entertain royalty. But I had put on a clean T-shirt myself, I must admit. I didn't want this blonde queen looking at me as if I were some kind of freak.

Andrew checked his hair one last time in the hall mirror and took off with the car keys, looking nervous and excited.

Daniel came downstairs wearing his bright blue sweatshirt that says QUESTION AUTHORITY. I helped Mom peel the sweet potatoes and watched her glaze them and stick them in the oven. This was going to be a great meal. It was as if we were all celebrating because Mom felt better.

Daniel poked his nose in the kitchen and cheered when he found out we were having eggplant. He would like to have eggplant every day. He won't eat green vegetables. Except artichokes.

Daddy had the fire going and the Levelors closed and some of the lights on. The living room really looked neat. Mom's blanket chest, which belonged to her great-grandmother, gleamed from the polish Andrew had given it. The wall-hanging that Daddy bought in Hungary matched the dark reds and blues and greens in the braided rugs. I hoped Bonnie Whoever would appreciate this house.

Terry, who had been looking out the hall window, shrieked, "Here they come! Here they come! Andrew ran over the curb."

"Oh, no," Daddy said.

"Chip off the old block," Mom said, and smiled and gave him a quick hug. "Remember, children, Andrew wants to make a good impression. Let's be on our best behavior."

I saw Andrew first. He was leading the way. I couldn't believe how he looked. Pink in the face and rattled. One small piece of hair at the back of his head was standing up straight. He stood in the doorway and coughed. My cool brother!

"Hi," he said to us, his own family, as if we were people he hardly knew, as if he hadn't just been with us. "Uh, Bonnie, this is my family. Family, this is Bonnie."

She stepped forward, smiling. She looked like a model. Red-headed. Tall. Slender. Slathered with makeup. Eye shadow a foot thick. Lipstick that made her look half dead. I hated her.

glaze them and stick them in the oven. This was going to be a great meal. It was as if we were all celebrating because Mom felt better.

Daniel poked his nose in the kitchen and cheered when he found out we were having eggplant. He would like to have eggplant every day. He won't eat green vegetables. Except artichokes.

Daddy had the fire going and the Levelors closed and some of the lights on. The living room really looked neat. Mom's blanket chest, which belonged to her great-grandmother, gleamed from the polish Andrew had given it. The wall-hanging that Daddy bought in Hungary matched the dark reds and blues and greens in the braided rugs. I hoped Bonnie Whoever would appreciate this house.

Terry, who had been looking out the hall window, shrieked, "Here they come! Here they come! Andrew ran over the curb."

"Oh, no," Daddy said.

"Chip off the old block," Mom said, and smiled and gave him a quick hug. "Remember, children, Andrew wants to make a good impression. Let's be on our best behavior."

I saw Andrew first. He was leading the way. I couldn't believe how he looked. Pink in the face and rattled. One small piece of hair at the back of his head was standing up straight. He stood in the doorway and coughed. My cool brother!

"Hi," he said to us, his own family, as if we were people he hardly knew, as if he hadn't just been with us. "Uh, Bonnie, this is my family. Family, this is Bonnie."

She stepped forward, smiling. She looked like a model. Red-headed. Tall. Slender. Slathered with makeup. Eye shadow a foot thick. Lipstick that made her look half dead. I hated her.

Chapter Six

I TRIED TO CONCENTRATE on how good the food was, but I couldn't. Mom was getting that tight look around her mouth that meant a headache was starting. I couldn't believe nobody else noticed it.

And there was my brother, whom I'd always looked up to, making a complete ass of himself. "Bonnie, have some cranberry sauce; Bonnie, have some more sweet potatoes . . ." Never mind that she already had some.

But the worst thing was the way he acted about us, as if we were this quaint, amusing, impossible bunch he'd been saddled with.

I began to think then for the first time about how soon Andrew would grow up and go away. I felt as if I were losing my family, right there under my eyes. I didn't think I could stand it.

This Bonnie gushed a lot. How wonderful the

food was. What a beautiful house it was. How cute Terry was. And Terry played up to that to the point of nausea. When she put her Parker House roll on top of her head and said she was the queen, Bonnie said, "Oh, how adorable."

I looked at Andrew. Normally he would say, "Mom, can't you control that revolting child?" But instead he said, "Terry's the family clown." As if that was just about the greatest thing a little kid could be.

Mom's voice was sharp. "Terry, stop that at once or you'll have to leave the table." Sharp was not what she usually was. It meant her head ached.

"Oh, don't send her away," Bonnie said. That was interfering with family discipline, which is against the rules in our house. But Mom let it go.

When Bonnie started beaming at Daniel, I could tell he felt like throwing up. But for a minute he was saved by Terry, who couldn't stand to lose Bonnie's attention. "Daniel is going to give me the Kanakeens," she said in a loud voice.

Daniel looked appalled. The Kanakeens were imaginary tiny people whom Daniel invented when he was about three or four years old. He was always yelling at us not to step on them. It got pretty nerve-wracking sometimes. But he had long since outgrown them.

Bonnie was saying to Terry, "What are Kanakeens, honey?"

Andrew had the grace to look embarrassed. "Oh,

they were these invisible people Daniel played with when he was little." I could tell he wanted to drop the subject, but Bonnie wasn't about to let anybody off the hook.

"Tell me about them," she said to Daniel. "I love imaginary friends, don't you?" That question was aimed at me.

"No," I said.

Andrew glared at me.

Mom was beginning to look distraught. I wanted to tell her to go lie down and I'd clear the dishes and get dessert and all, but I knew she'd hate to have me call attention to how she felt, especially with a guest there.

"So Daniel just leaves them in his bureau drawer," Terry said. "So I can have them. It's dark in there. They don't like it."

"Oh, I love it," Bonnie said, beaming at Daniel as if he were just the cutest little leprechaun.

He had his chin down on his chest, and he was staring at the sugar bowl. His glasses slid down his nose.

"I recall," said Daddy who hadn't spoken for a while, "that Andrew stepped on one once and burst into tears when Dan said he'd killed it."

Andrew turned bright red. "I was just kidding," he muttered.

"It's hard to kid yourself into bursting into tears," I said. No one paid any attention.

"You have to open doors for them," Terry said.

4 3

"They're too little to reach the knob." She was leaning toward Bonnie, to get her attention.

"I'd love to meet them some time," Bonnie said. She had a spot of cranberry sauce on her chin and she didn't even know it.

Daddy cleared his throat. "Would you like some more turkey, Bonnie? A bit of nice crusty wing?" He smiled at her, but he was hiding behind the beard. I can always tell.

She took the bit of nice crusty wing. For such a delicate, angel-like female, she had a whale of an appetite. Maybe she spent all the family income on cashmere sweaters and they were starving.

Terry banged her spoon against her plate to make us listen. "Daniel's got a hundred and forty cats," she said.

Daniel glared at her.

"Darling, you're not making sense," Mom said. "Drink your milk."

"A hundred and forty cats," Daddy said. "What on earth do you suppose that means?"

"A hundred and forty Q's," Terry said. "He told Uncle Walt. I heard him."

"Well, let's straighten that out later," Mom said. "Daniel, dear, eat your dinner."

He looked at her, and then he said in a clear voice, "She means I've got an IQ of a hundred and forty."

"That's what I said," Terry said.

Andrew hooted. "That's a fantasy; that *is* a fantasy." He leaned toward Bonnie. "My little brother is about to flunk third grade. A hundred forty IQ, wow! How's that for dreaming!" He sounded mean. I had never heard Andrew sound mean before, especially to Daniel.

Daniel looked as if he might cry. He was starting to push his chair back, but Daddy put his hand out and stopped him.

"Eat your dinner," he said.

I couldn't stand it. I said, "It's true. Mr. Hergesheimer said Daniel has a near-genius IQ. A hundred and forty. I heard him say it."

There was total silence. Then Andrew said, kind of weakly, "Come on, Kit." But Andrew knows I don't tell lies.

"Is that true, son?" Daddy said to Daniel.

"Yes," Daniel said. He was looking at me in an odd way, kind of triumphant, and as if he really liked me.

"Well!" Daddy said. "That's a shocker."

"It's wonderful," Mom said. "We'll have to talk about it later. Kit, Andrew, Daniel, help clear the dishes please."

In the kitchen I saw Mom give Daniel a quick hug and whisper something to him. He smiled.

After dinner Mom went up to her room. I washed the dishes. Bonnie and Andrew were in the basement listening to tapes. Or something. I checked on Mom, but she was lying on her bed with her clothes on and her eyes shut. I wished she would open her eyes and smile at me, just for a second. But she didn't. I don't know if she even knew I was there.

I went to my room and turned on the public radio station. It was the Chicago Symphony. I tried to listen and forget everybody, especially Bonnie and Andrew. "This is my sister-in-law, Bonnie Esterly. Bonnie Esterly." I felt like gagging.

I concentrated on my Chinese girl. What should I name her? What were some Chinese girls' names? How about Li? No. How about Anna? Anna Wong? Anna Wong is thirteen years old. She is small and dark with an oval face and interesting slanted eyes like Chu Vang, the Vietnamese boy in our class. She looks mysterious, but she gets scared and worried just the way I do.

I got my legal pad and began making notes. Pretty soon there was a knock on my door. I thought it was Daniel so I said, "Give the password and enter." But it was Bonnie. I stuck the legal pad under the blanket.

"I'm leaving," she said. "I just wanted to say good-bye."

"Good-bye," I said.

She went on standing there. And she looked different. I wondered what she and Andrew had been doing down in the basement. I didn't want to think about it, but I couldn't help it. I guess I might have glared at her, although I didn't do it on purpose.

She hung there in the doorway as if she couldn't move. Nobody said anything for a long minute. Then in a funny kind of voice that was different from the one she'd been using at dinner, she said, "I'm sorry you don't like me."

I felt my face get red. I didn't know what to do. She still didn't move. Finally I said, "Who said I didn't?"

She blinked a couple of times. I thought it must be an effort to blink with all that mascara hanging on your eyelashes. "Good night, Kit," she said. And she left. Finally.

A few minutes later Terry came by and wanted me to read her asleep. I said I had a headache. I pretended to be asleep when Mom came in, but she knew I wasn't. She sat down on the bed.

"You weren't very nice to Andrew's friend," she said.

"Well, I didn't like her."

"She was a guest in our house. We are gracious to our guests whether we like them or not. And as far as liking goes, we can hardly know on the basis of a couple of hours whether we like someone or not, can we?"

"Andrew was acting like an idiot."

"Andrew was acting like a teen-aged boy. Before long you'll be acting like a teen-aged girl."

"Never."

Mom leaned down and kissed my cheek. "Good night, Kit. Sleep easy."

She was gone, and I hadn't even asked her how she felt.

Chapter
Seven

AT BREAKFAST I apologized to Andrew. He shrugged
and said, "Tell her, don't tell me." I didn't think that
was very gracious. If Mom had been there, she'd have
told him so, but she was sleeping in, and Daddy was
giving us breakfast. When we are all at breakfast together, there are five cereal boxes, from Daddy's Grape-
nuts to Terry's Captain Crunch. You can hardly see
anybody over the boxes. Nobody except Terry talks
much.

I was anxious to get to school to hear more about
the Visiting Author. The only person I was worried
about as competition was Chu Vang. He was new in
town and had started at our school in January. Nobody
knew him well at all. But lately he had been writing
some very good poetry and a couple of stories. Kind of

strange and exotic, but beautiful. My friend Anna had a crush on him, but I don't think he even noticed.

Mrs. Ramer told us that Miss Hortense Perry would be with us next week. Miss Hortense Perry was our Visiting Author, and she had been published in all kinds of literary magazines and once in *The New Yorker*. The fact that Mrs. Ramer called her *Miss* Perry made me think she must be oldish. If she was young, it would be Ms. So I pictured a white-haired lady, around sixty or seventy, with kindly blue eyes and an absentminded manner. Mrs. Ramer read us a couple of Miss Perry's nature poems. They were good, all right, but you couldn't tell from them how old she was. I asked Mrs. Ramer, and she said, "I really don't know, Katharine. Does it matter?" I think Mrs. Ramer is sensitive about age. She's pushing forty-five herself.

We were supposed to turn in by the end of the week whatever story or poem we wanted Miss Perry to judge. When Miss Perry got here, she would read them and decide who was the winner and who was the runner-up. Those two people would get private conferences and have their work published in the paper. Miss Perry would also have classes for everybody.

I couldn't wait to work on my story. I thought about it all the rest of the day. Miss Hugo got mad at me in Latin class because I wasn't listening to what she said about the ablative.

It was the first year our school had had Latin. It was part of a program the school board thought up called "Return to the Classics." My father approved of it. Most of the kids didn't like Latin, but I thought it was fun. I liked seeing how a lot of our words came from Latin.

After school I made excuses to Anna and the other kids who wanted me to play volleyball, and I told Daniel I wouldn't be going straight home. Instead, I headed for the Chinese cemetery. It seemed the best place to get my story straight in my head.

The sun was so warm, it felt like summer as I lay down on the pine needles near the sign that said this had been the Chinese cemetery. I could hear the rushing sound the river made down below. A robin was hopping around, and I wondered if they had robins in China. But if my heroine was born in this country, all she would know about China would be what her parents told her. She would hardly ever see her father because he would be off slaving on the railroad. He leaves the girl, whose name is . . . is what? Anna Wong? Would my friend Anna be mad if I used her first name? She might think I was saying she was really Chinese. I would like it if somebody thought I was Chinese, but I didn't think Anna would. But now I had Anna Wong stuck in my mind. Anyway this father leaves Anna and her mother in our town, and they are terribly poor and live in a tiny shack on the other side of the river. Something terrible happens, and Anna has to cross the river during spring flood to get help. There isn't any bridge, except maybe a little footbridge that is washed away by the river. So what happened that makes her risk her life crossing the river? Maybe the shack burned down?

I flopped over on my stomach and the pine needles tickled my face. It smelled wonderful. There was no breeze at all. Some kind of bird was chirping in the trees, and there was a squirrel making chirpy noises, not bird-chirpy, but that kind of little squeak a frying pan makes rubbing against another pot. I thought myself into Anna. She was lying here, and she was lonely and scared. Other kids made fun of her because she was different. Little boys pulled her braids. She had these very black braids and black, snapping eyes.

I woke up when the squirrel knocked a pine cone off the tree and it fell on my head. I couldn't believe I'd gone to sleep, right when I was creating my story. I'll bet Miss Hortense Perry doesn't fall asleep in the middle of a poem. Maybe I'm not a truly dedicated writer after all.

The sun had gone behind some clouds, and it was a lot cooler. I got up and walked home. Maybe Uncle Walt could tell me some good background stuff for my Chinese girl. I guess he wasn't old enough to have been here when the railroad was built, but he's been to China.

I tried to think of an opening sentence. Mrs. Ramer says the opening sentence is the most important one in a story. "Anna Wong stared in terror at the rising river." "Anna Wong's black eyes were horrified as she watched the river rush past her. A huge log was tossed around on the foaming water like a matchstick." "Anna Wong caught her breath in fright as . . ."

The minute I came into our yard, I knew something was wrong. Daddy's car was there, parked all slanty as if he'd been in a hurry. I could hear Terry crying at the top of her lungs. Daniel's bike was on the grass, not in the garage where he always puts it. My heart began to pound.

Andrew was standing in the middle of the kitchen as if he didn't know what to do next. Daniel was leaning against the wall sipping a glass of milk. No sandwich. Terry was bellowing.

"Where's Daddy?" I said.

Andrew took a long breath. "He took Mom to the hospital."

I sat down. My knees were acting funny. "Why?"

Andrew looked pale. "The doctor wants to give her some tests. Just some tests, that's all."

"A brain scan," Daniel said.

Terry's voice rose even higher.

"Shut up, Terry," I said. I guess I scared her. She stopped right in the middle of a scream. The kitchen got still as death. "Why?" I said to Andrew.

"To see what's causing her headaches."

"She just has headaches." I heard myself sounding mad, but I wasn't sure who I was mad at. Maybe Doctor Fuller? Maybe Mom?

"This one was worse. I came home and found her

moaning and everything. It was awful." Andrew sounded scared, just remembering it. "I called Daddy, and he called Doctor Fuller. Daddy came tearing home, and they took her to the hospital in Doctor Fuller's car." Then he added, "He's got a Continental." As if that had anything to do with anything.

"How long will she be there?"

Andrew shrugged. "Till they find out what's wrong."

"There's nothing wrong with Mom's brain," I said. "That's silly."

Suddenly Andrew was mad at me. "So you know more than the doctors and the machines and all the experts."

"I know Mama."

"What's for dinner?" Daniel said.

I wanted to hit him, but then I glanced at him and saw how worried he looked. He was just trying to get us to stop talking about Mama.

"I'll fix something," I said. "There's roast beef left. And a little of the turkey."

"Don't let Mrs. Hume come," Daniel said.

"Cranberry sauce?" Terry said. She kept hiccuping from crying so hard.

I looked at them. They were all watching me. Somebody had to do something, and I guess it was me. What would Anna Wong do? I couldn't save the family by crossing the river at flood stage. But maybe I could tide them over by fixing a good dinner. There's a time to cry and a time to cook. Had I read that somewhere or did I make it up?

"Andrew, will you carve both the beef and the turkey? As long as everybody doesn't want the same thing, there'll be plenty. Dan, if you want to slice the eggplant, I'll make a sauce to bake it in." I knew he'd be happy about having eggplant. "Terry . . . why don't you get the Kanakeens all together so nobody will step on them and tell them a bedtime story?"

Terry thought about it. "All right, but they're all over the house. I've told them and told them to stick together, but they don't listen." She scampered off to round up Kanakeens. That would take her quite a while.

"Dad said not to wait dinner for him," Andrew told me. He was picking out his favorite carving knife. He and Dad have a thing about the right knife for the right chore. "He'll call us later."

Daniel was washing and peeling the eggplant. "I can't find Mr. Quickly," he said.

I looked at Andrew, who frowned and looked away. "He'll show up, Dan," I said.

Andrew cut carefully into the beef. "He got scared and tore off when there was all that confusion getting Mom into the car. He'll be back."

"I know that," Daniel said. But he went on looking worried.

I washed some mushrooms for the tomato sauce for the eggplant, all the time trying not to think about Mom in the hospital. I hated hospitals. I had my tonsils out when I was six, and there was a faded bloodstain on my hospital shirt. I thought it was chocolate pudding. What an icky thing to think. And why did they have a stained shirt on me anyway? Maybe it was my own blood. I do not like blood. There wouldn't be any blood in a brain scan. I started to ask Andrew what happened in a brain scan anyway, but I couldn't make myself say it. Right then I cut my thumb. You can't get away from blood.

Chapter Eight

DINNER WAS STRANGE. Daddy hadn't come, and somehow without planning it, Andrew and I began to sound like parents. I heard myself telling Terry to chew her food before she swallowed it, just the way Mom does. And Andrew was listening patiently to Daniel's story of why he had almost flunked Mr. Hergesheimer's geography test. It seems he spent nearly the whole period writing a long explanation to Mr. Hergesheimer of why his question about the islands of the Caribbean was "ambitious."

Andrew looked puzzled and then said, "Ambiguous?"

"Whatever," Daniel said.

Terry started complaining that one of the Kanakeens was missing, and she couldn't go to sleep till he was found.

Andrew said to me, "She's worse than Dan ever was."

I had a feeling it was Mom that Terry was missing. Daniel gave me a look, and I knew he thought that, too. Sometimes Daniel and I are on exactly the same wavelength.

"I know where he is, Terry," he said.

"Where?" Terry looked suspicious.

"He's the one that hides inside the roll of toilet paper under the bathroom sink."

"He couldn't get in. It's wrapped in plastic stuff."

"He figured that out long ago. He gets the manicure scissors and punches a tiny little hole that's big enough to let him in."

Terry looked as if she didn't believe it.

"He can hardly lift those huge scissors, but he does it; and that's where he is."

Terry slid out of her chair, and Andrew said, "You haven't been excused, Terry."

I thought if what's-her-name wanted to know how he'd look and act when he was a father, she should be here now.

Terry's face screwed up for a big wail, so I said to Andrew quickly, "I'll help her find the Kanakeen and then give her a bath and put her to bed."

Andrew looked relieved. Not only to get rid of Terry but to get himself off the hook about making her stay at the table. Mom and Daddy have the authority for that kind of stuff, but Andrew and I don't. Lately

I feel like a twelve-year-old housewife, but I don't really have the clout.

"Please excuse me," Daniel said. "I have to look for Q. I'll do the dishes when I get back."

"It's my turn," Andrew said.

"I'll help."

We were all being so good, it was a real strain. I was thankful when Terry was finally in bed. It takes longer than I ever think it will to get her there. She knows of more ways to stall than most people could think up, though Mom says I was pretty good at it, too. With Terry, there's the Raggedy Ann stall, and the Cabbage Patch doll stall, and another wait for finding Alice, the china doll with the front teeth that got broken when Terry forced a pretzel into her mouth. And there's the glass of water. You get her water and she drinks it all right down, so you have to get her some more.

By the time I got downstairs, the boys had done the dishes and Daniel had gone out again to look for his cat. He came back just as Daddy drove in. He—Daniel— looked as if he'd been crying. It didn't seem fair that he had to lose his cat now.

Daddy said, "Well." And we waited, scared to hear whatever he was going to say. He looked exhausted. "Well, they did a lot of tests. They'll do some more in the morning." He leaned back in his chair as if he was too tired to sit up. "Doctor Fuller is having a consultation in the morning with a very good neurosurgeon."

"Surgeon!" Andrew said.

"Yes. Well, they aren't sure, but she may have a small tumor."

"Where?" Daniel said.

Daddy didn't want to answer. But finally he said, "On the brain."

I started to cry. Andrew got up and looked out the window, as if he expected to find answers out there in the trees. Daniel was sitting perfectly still. His eyes were huge.

"Now then," Daddy said, making his voice brisk, "I'm sure it will be all right. Your mother is a strong woman . . ." His voice broke, and his eyes filled with tears. "We just have to be brave and pray hard." He got up and took his coffee cup into the kitchen.

"There's no sense crying," Andrew said to me. "She'll be all right. She's bound to be. People get tumors removed from their brains all the time, and they're just fine."

I went up to my room. There's a place where it's no good trying to be brave. Then you get by that place and begin again.

I couldn't go to sleep. I turned on the radio low, but they were just finishing *Encores by Request,* and then they started a rock program. I like rock sometimes, but not then. I shut it off and sat on my window seat for a while staring at the stars and wondering what it was all about.

I heard a little sound outside my door. When I opened it, Daniel was there in his pajamas, huddled against the wall with Lamb in his lap. He was asleep. I picked him up and took him back to his bed. He almost woke up. He half opened his eyes and said, " 'Night, Mom."

In my room I turned on the light and got my yellow legal pad and my favorite purple Pilot pen. I thought for a long time, then I wrote, "The river had never looked so dangerous."

Chapter
Nine

It had been a terrible week. Andrew hadn't played his guitar since the day Mom went to the hospital. Daniel's cat hadn't come back. And Terry kept losing Kanakeens until I thought I'd scream. When you're coming downstairs and this child shrieks at you, "Look where you're stepping! You broke his neck!" it's pretty unnerving. Especially if you're unnerved anyway.

The doctors had agreed that Mom had a tumor, and they were going to operate on Saturday. We could not go to see her because children aren't allowed in the hospital. She sent us little notes, and we sent her little notes. And we were scared.

We had persuaded Daddy not to call Mrs. Hume about dinner, but thinking of things to make was getting hard. A couple of times Andrew just went to the

Bar MG and brought home Trail Boss sandwiches for all of us. We ate a lot of potato chips.

I got my story done. It was about this Chinese girl whose mother gets very sick, like an attack of appendicitis that she could die of if somebody didn't get help. And Anna Wong has to cross the river, which is at flood stage, to bring help.

The day I finished it, I went up the mountain to Uncle Walt's bench. I wasn't sure why I wanted to see him, except that he seems kind of eternal and safe. I found Daniel there, and he had been crying. He left right after I came.

"Why was Daniel crying?" As if I didn't know. He kept Lamb with him all the time except for school. And he had been reading about the brain in one of Dad's books. Besides, Mr. Q had not come back.

"He worries," Uncle Walt said. "About his mother. And about his cat." He peeled the banana Daniel had brought him and offered me half. "I would like to take him rafting this weekend, if your father doesn't mind."

I guess I was still thinking of the flooded river in my story. I said, "Oh, please don't. He'll drown."

He looked at me in the thoughtful way he has, as if he's considering what you've said from all angles. "Troubles don't necessarily come in groups," he said. His voice was very gentle. "But if it worries you, I surely won't. Perhaps we could go to the ice cream parlor instead." He meant the Dairy Queen.

"Mama gets operated on, on Saturday," I said.

"I know."

"Uncle Walt, have you known anybody who got that kind of operation?"

"Yes. Three people, in fact."

"What happened?"

"Two of them recovered very nicely. One died."

I felt as if he had stuck a knife in me. "That's not a very nice thing to say."

He reached out and took my hand. "You asked me, Katharine. I don't lie to you. It was some years ago that that man died. I'm sure the operation is much improved." He let go of my hand and seemed to forget me for a while. Then he said, "Death is not a terrible thing, you know. It may in fact be quite wonderful. Considering how astonishing life is."

"She's not your mother."

"No. That's true." He was silent again, and I was thinking of leaving. He said, "If your father wouldn't mind, I'd like to come and cook dinner for you Saturday night. Daniel tells me you children have been doing it. It must get rather hard on you."

For some reason I felt better. As if a good meal could change anything.

On the way home I passed a woman riding a horse up the trail, and I got to thinking about how Mom and Aunt Geraldine used to do trick riding at county fairs. I guess they were really good. We have pictures of them.

64

After Andrew was born, Aunt Geraldine was killed when a horse threw her off, and Mom never rode again. Andrew is the only one of us kids who likes horses. I'm scared of them, and Daniel is allergic to them.

When I got home, Daddy had just come from the hospital, and he looked like a thundercloud. I was afraid to ask what was wrong, what *else* was wrong.

At dinner, which was steak, he said, "Your mother's operation has been postponed until next week."

Everybody got very tense.

"Why?" Andrew said finally.

"They want to do some more studies. They've called in another specialist from Spokane. I know it's hard on all of us, but we'll just have to stay cheerful." He grinned like a Halloween pumpkin, and his teeth were white as gravestones.

Nobody said anything for a while. Then Andrew said I had cooked his steak too much, and I said, "Cook it yourself then."

Daniel said, "Mr. Quickly hasn't come back." He looked so desolate, I felt like crying.

The small radio was on, and the newsman was talking about a man who was held up by two guys outside a bar downtown, and he shot one of them dead and wounded the other.

"Good for him," I said, and Daddy looked at me with what I think of as Pennsylvania horror.

"What a barbaric thing to say!"

6 5

"Well, people have to defend themselves," I said. I know good and well that *I* wouldn't shoot anybody, but the principle seemed okay.

"If people start breaking down law and order," Daddy said, "we will soon have no civilization left."

I felt like arguing. "We don't have much anyway." I should have shut up. I could see I was upsetting him. But we were all so upset anyway, nothing would have smoothed things down.

His voice sounded funny, kind of choked. "You Montanans," he said. "You're all vigilantes at heart."

Andrew and I looked at each other, and Andrew began to laugh. "Come on, Dad," he said, "we're *your* kids too."

"I'm your kid, Daddy," Terry said, in her most cajoling voice. She ran around the table and climbed into his lap.

"I hate violence!" he said violently. He put Terry down and got up from the table. His eyes were full of tears. He walked away without even saying excuse me.

"Poor Daddy," Daniel said.

I began to cry, too. I couldn't help it. Tears streaked down my face. Andrew reached his long arm across the table and gave me a whack on the wrist that was supposed to be affectionate, I guess.

"Go tell him you're sorry," he said.

"I'm not sorry."

"Sure you are. It isn't the stupid gunman you're both crying about. It's Mom."

That made me really cry. I went into Daddy's study. He was sitting there with his legs stretched out in front of him, staring out the window. I put my arms around his neck and kissed him somewhere near his ear. Kissing a beard is always a funny experience. I said, "I'm sorry."

"Oh, Kit," he said. He put his arms around me, and both of us cried.

Chapter Ten

ON SATURDAY Andrew and I got to see Mom. Doctor Fuller made special arrangements for us. I was so excited, I felt nauseated. And when we walked into Mom's room and saw her sitting up in a chair looking perfectly okay, I thought I'd faint.

Both of us were shy with her, as if she had become somebody strange that we almost but not quite knew. I guess I stared at her because she laughed and said, "It's only me, Kit."

Andrew said, very formally, "How are you feeling?"

"Quite good, sweetie. How are you? Tell me about Daniel and Terry and yourselves. Has Daniel found Mr. Q?"

"He never came back," Andrew said.

"Oh, poor Daniel. Kit, do you think we should get him a kitten?"

I had been thinking about that myself, but I wasn't sure Daniel would want another cat. "It might make him feel worse."

"Q might still come back. He ran away two years ago and was gone a week," Andrew said.

We had so many things to talk about, the twenty minutes flew by. Mom wanted to know about the Visiting Author and how my story was coming, and how Andrew's girl was.

"Bonnie?" he said, looking vague. "Oh, we broke up."

"Broke up!" I was shocked. "How could you do that?"

But the nurse came in then to say it was time for us to go. As I kissed Mom goodbye, it suddenly hit me that she could die before I ever saw her again. I had trouble getting out of there without bursting into tears.

I took it out on Andrew. "How could you break up with Bonnie? Just days ago you were drooling all over her . . ."

"That's enough, Kit," Daddy said.

"What do you care?" Andrew said. "You didn't even like her."

"I never said I didn't like her."

"Actions speak louder than words."

"Stop it," Daddy said. "It's none of your business, Kit."

We both sulked all the way home. And when we got there, Daniel was out hunting for his cat again. He had been all around the neighborhood knocking on doors to see if Mr. Q might have gotten shut in somebody's garage, as he did once, or even if someone had just seen him. Every day he called the radio station and got them to announce: "Lost, a male cat, four years old, in the Lower Rattlesnake, silver with black stripes and green eyes. Answers to the name of Mr. Quickly, or just Q. Call Daniel Esterly at 721-5129. Reward." We kept getting calls, but it was usually somebody who had seen a black cat with silver stripes, or a female cat with blue eyes, or just a kid trying to claim the reward. Which, as I happened to know, was one Kennedy silver dollar, a Finnish pennia from Daddy's sabbatical, and ten very old baseball cards, which Uncle Walt had given him. Those were Daniel's most treasured possessions. Except Lamb, whom he would never give up.

Andrew and I stopped being mad at each other because we were worried about Daniel. He was so sad. Andrew got the idea of distracting him by offering a dollar fifty for every A he got before the end of school. I offered to pay half. When we told Daniel, he thought about it for a few minutes, and then he sighed and said, "All right. I could use the money to buy Mama a present."

Then Uncle Walt showed up, and I was embarrassed because I had forgotten he was coming. He didn't mind though. He settled into the kitchen as if he had always lived there, and he wouldn't let any of us help him. "The whole point is, you get some time to do your own things. Katharine, I expect you'll want to work on your story."

I didn't know he even knew about my story. Daniel must have told him. It made me feel famous, like notes in the *New York Times* that say, "Eudora Welty is working on a new collection of stories."

When I came downstairs at dinnertime, Daddy was sitting in the kitchen smoking his pipe and looking relaxed for the first time in days. They were talking about the City Council and its mistakes.

"You ought to run, Walter," Daddy said. "You've got more sense than anybody in town."

"Thanks." Uncle Walt laughed, what I would call a satirical laugh. "I can see it now. 'Retired hobo and world wanderer runs for City Council. His slogan is, Straighten out and fly right.' "

"I'd vote for you," Daniel said. He had just come in from Q-hunting. "Did anybody call?"

"One young gentleman who wanted to know how much the reward was. I told him to produce the cat and he'd find out," Daddy said.

Daniel looked anxious. "Do you think he has him?"

"No, I do not."

"How do you know?"

"There were raucous voices in the background egging him on. I suspect it was your friend Tony."

Daniel looked shocked. "He wouldn't do that."

Daddy backtracked. "No, I'm sure it was just some kid."

The dinner was wonderful. Uncle Walt had broiled salmon steaks, which a friend had caught on the Washington coast. And there were boiled new potatoes with butter and parsley, garden tomatoes, radishes and little green onions from the Farmers' Market. And artichoke hearts for Daniel. And garlic toast.

Uncle Walt got Daniel to talk for the first time in days. He sounded almost like his old self, wanting to know what God was doing before the Big Bang. Nobody could tell him, so Uncle Walt told us about diatoms, little microscopic creatures that create perfect glass hexagons.

Over dessert, three flavors of ice cream, Uncle Walt talked about his travels, especially in Burma. He had been married then, and his wife Bertha went with him. He never said very much about her, but you could tell he still loved her. She'd died when their only child was born, and the baby died, too. It was very sad.

He told us about meeting General Stilwell after the general's famous trek over the Burma Road. When he finished, he stopped and gazed into space and said, "It seems like yesterday." Then he kind of shook himself and told a funny story.

I hated to see Uncle Walt leave. While he was there, we felt better, but then he was gone and we were all conscious of the empty space where our mother would be if she were okay.

I said I thought the dinner was wonderful. I guess I was trying to hold onto the good feeling Uncle Walt had brought us.

Daniel said, "I think the toast was slightly over-garlicked."

He was making a little joke. For Daniel you can't over-garlic anything. We all laughed more than we would have ordinarily.

Later I heard him in the yard calling Q. I had a feeling he was calling Mom at the same time, and I could hardly stand it.

When he was in bed, he showed me a note Mom had sent him that said, "Daniel dear, it occurred to me that you might make a little song out of the names of the tests I've had. So far I've had CAT, PET, EEG, and BEAM. I love you. Mom."

He had written a lot of words and crossed them out, and what he had left was: "My pet cat is asleep in a moonbeam. A mouse runs past his nose. He wakes up fast and says EEG, EEG, and that's how my song goes."

"It's just a rough draft," Daniel said.

"It's fine," I said.

He looked up at me. His face was pale. "Q will come home, won't he?"

I said, "I don't know, Dan."

He winced, and I felt as if I had betrayed him. What would Mom have said? I can't help it if I'm not wise enough to know the right answers.

"We're all praying for him," I said, and kissed his forehead to say good night.

I decided I would go to the animal shelter and get him a kitten. It was the only thing I could think of to do.

Chapter
Eleven

On Monday Mrs. Ramer introduced Miss Hortense Perry to our class. It was a real shock. Miss Hortense Perry is about twenty-eight years old. She is tall and skinny with very crinkly red hair that comes way below her waist. When you look at her, all you register is HAIR. It looks as if any minute it might fly right out as if she'd had an electric charge.

Otherwise, she has pale blue eyes and freckles and wire-rimmed glasses, what Daddy says they used to call Ben Franklin glasses. She is very tense, and she gestures a lot, kind of uncontrolled gestures that knock papers off desks.

She talked a few minutes about how wonderful poetry is and how glad she is to be exploring its wonders with us, and she assured us she was going to read our contributions that night and by Tuesday she would let us know who the winner was.

We clapped; and she made a gesture like an opera singer taking a bow and knocked Mrs. Ramer's stapler onto the floor. When she leaned over to pick it up, she bumped her head. Is this what it means to be a poet?

I was in a hurry to get away from school because I was going to the animal shelter, and it's quite a long way. While Mom was gone, Mrs. Hume was keeping Terry at her house till I get home. I gave Daniel a key to the house. Andrew was playing baseball.

Anna wanted to know where I was going, but I didn't tell her. I hadn't told anyone, because there might not be a suitable kitten, and then Daniel would be disappointed. I was sure he would be pleased to get a kitten, because it was getting pretty obvious that Mr. Q was not coming home.

On the way out, I reminded Daniel that I would be late.

"I know. I'm a latchkey kid." He seemed to like the idea.

I wasn't sure if you had to pay for a kitten at the shelter or not, but I had three dollars plus bus fare.

I was almost out the door when Mr. Hergesheimer caught up with me. "Katharine," he said, "I don't know what's come over Daniel, but . . ."

I interrupted him. If I missed the bus, there wouldn't be another one for forty-five minutes. "He can't help it, Mr. Hergesheimer. Our mother is going to have an operation, and we're all very worried."

"My dear child, I know that. And I'm so sorry. Mrs. Hergesheimer and I are praying for her."

I was trying to imagine Mr. Hergesheimer with a Mrs. Hergesheimer, praying for my mother. I had never thought of him outside the third grade.

He said, "I wanted to tell you that Daniel is doing splendidly. He has had A's in the two tests I gave this week. I don't know what's come over him, but I'm delighted."

I felt like saying, "One fifty an A is what's come over him," but I just thanked him and said that was fine. Bribery pays.

I just barely made the bus. I had my mother's straw gardening hat with me, because you're not supposed to have animals on the bus, and I thought I could stash the kitten away in the hat. It's a tall hat.

It was about a half mile walk from the bus to the animal shelter. I'd never been there before. It was a long, low cinder block building, and when I got close, I could hear dogs barking.

Practically as soon as I got inside, I wanted to take home all the cats and dogs I could see. They looked at me as if they expected it or hoped for it, like orphans. Some of them looked very sad, others bounced around and barked or meowed as the case might be. I fell in love with a funny puppy that looked like a white dust mop.

And there was a wonderful big white cat with blue eyes, who looked like a queen inspecting a peasant who'd come to ask a favor.

A feisty little terrier was barking so loudly, I had trouble telling the woman in charge what I wanted. She was nice. She told me to look around, and she pointed out the kittens. There was a family of three kittens that I hadn't even noticed at first. She said they were old enough to be adopted. One was golden, one was pure white, and the third one was part gold, part white. I wished I could take them all.

When I put my hand in the cage, the white one arched her back and spat at me. It made me laugh, she was so little. It took me quite a while to make up my mind. The lady said there were some other kittens out back, but I thought I should decide on one of these. If I looked at six or eight, it would be six or eight times as hard to make up my mind.

Finally I knew I had to make up my mind and get out of there. I felt like crying over all those nice animals that nobody wanted. The gold kitten was kind of sedate, and I worried that she might not be healthy. The little white one with the blue eyes bit my finger and glared at me. I knew how she felt. I was invading her space. The orange and white one was a male, and if Mr. Q should ever come back, he'd be angry to find another male cat. I told the lady I'd take the white one.

She said it was a good choice. She took the kitten

out and handed it to me. The kitten stared hard at me and then seemed to decide she'd put up with me after all. She curled into a little ball in my hands.

I put her in my mother's hat, and I gave the woman all the money I had with me, except busfare. You don't have to pay for a kitten, but I thought it might help buy food for the other animals. "I hope somebody takes that white shaggy puppy," I said.

"I'm sure they will. He's a sweet dog, and young and healthy. And very appealing."

I said goodbye to her and to the dust mop puppy and to my kitten's siblings. Luckily we didn't have to wait long for a bus. I held the brim of the hat bunched together, so the bus man wouldn't notice, and I sat at the back of the bus.

At first the kitten slept. But when we were about a half mile from our street, she suddenly jumped out of the hat and leaped up on the shoulder of a man in front of us who was half asleep. I made a grab for the kitten, but she jumped down into his lap. That was the most surprised-looking man I ever saw. He stared at her, and she stared at him. I was praying the bus driver wasn't looking in his big mirror. I said, "Excuse me," and took the kitten out of the man's lap.

He looked at me as if he thought he was dreaming. Then he grinned. "I'll be darned," he said.

I put the kitten back in the hat, and I didn't think the driver had seen her, but when I got off, he said, "Show her who's boss, or she'll run you ragged."

I was so surprised, I said, "Thank you," and got off as fast as I could.

The kitchen door, which is the one we mostly use, was locked. It scared me. I was afraid something had happened to Daniel. He should have been home long before. I knocked, in case he'd locked it from the inside for some reason. After a minute he came around the back of the house. He looked hot and upset.

"What's the matter?"

"I lost the key."

"Oh, no!" Daddy and Andrew had keys, but I had given him mine. Daddy and Andrew wouldn't be home for another hour or so. "How could you do that?"

"That's a silly question. Tony is trying to get in through Mr. Q's entrance. You'd better come help me push him." He hadn't noticed the kitten. I put her on the front porch and closed the screen door so she couldn't get out, then followed Daniel around to the far side of the house. And there was Tony on his stomach, with his head out of sight somewhere inside the little trap door that Q used to come in and out.

Daniel knelt beside him and began to push him forward by his feet. "Help push," he said to me.

"Dan, he's going to get stuck. He can't get through that little door."

"He's skinny. He can make it. Help me."

So I knelt down and grabbed Tony's knees and

8 o

tried to push him forward. At first he moved along, inch by inch.

"He's making it," Daniel said. He was red in the face from pushing.

Tony said something, but his voice was muffled, and I didn't get what he said.

"His head is the biggest thing," Daniel said, "and that's through."

"His shoulders are the widest."

Tony yelled, and this time you couldn't not hear him. "I'm stuck!"

"Let all your breath out," Daniel told him. "Don't breathe."

"Get me out of here." Tony sounded as if he might start wailing in a minute.

"Couldn't you get in through a window?" I asked Daniel.

"All locked." He gave a hard push, and Tony yelled.

"Wait, Dan. This is not working." I tried to think. I knew he was right about the windows. Since Daddy got his home computer, he locks the place up like a prison. "We'll just have to wait till Andrew or Daddy get here."

Tony was banging his feet up and down and making anguished noises.

"He swelled up, that's what's wrong," Daniel said. He was studying Tony's wiggly body as if it were a math

8 1

problem. "I measured him and I measured the door. He should've been able to make it."

"Well, obviously he can't." I began pulling Tony out. But after a few seconds, he stopped coming. He really was stuck. I could imagine Tony's mother suing us. I didn't know what to do, and I began to get mad. "How could you lose the key? It was on a string around your neck."

"The string hurt my neck. So I put the key in my pocket."

"How could you be so irresponsible!"

"Stop talking like a grownup. Why didn't you come home and take care of us the way you're supposed to?"

"I'm not supposed to! I'm not your mother."

But Daniel never liked to fight. It struck him as a waste of time. "Tony," he said, "can you hear me?"

"Of course I can hear you. Get me out!" Tony was really yelling.

Suddenly I wanted to burst out laughing, but that would only have made them mad.

"Tip yourself on a slant," Daniel said to Tony. And to me he said, "Remember, like that chest of drawers Daddy got into Terry's bedroom?"

I remembered. It wouldn't go through straight up, so he finally got it through on a slant. It had been Mom's suggestion actually. Daddy had been trying to get it in by brute force.

Finally Daniel got his idea across to Tony. Tony

wiggled himself sort of half onto his side, and Dan and I pulled on his feet. He shot out of the hole, clean as a whistle.

"There you are." Daniel looked pleased with himself.

But Tony was not pleased. His face was dirty and tear-streaked, and his shirt was a mess. He ran off without saying goodbye.

"I don't know why he's so upset," Daniel said.

"Listen," I said, remembering the kitten, "I brought you something."

"I hope I can eat it. I'm starving."

I took him around to the front porch. The kitten reared up on her hind legs, batting her paw at a fly on the screen. "She's for you."

Daniel stared at her. "Thank you," he said. "But I don't want another cat." And he walked away.

I sat on the steps with the kitten in my lap. I felt as if I didn't even belong to this family.

Chapter Twelve

PEOPLE HAD DIFFERENT reactions to the kitten. Daddy looked dismayed, and when he heard that Daniel didn't want it, he said I'd better take it back. I felt like throwing a temper tantrum.

Andrew thought it was cute, but he had a date coming up with a new girl and he wasn't paying much attention to anything else.

Terry squealed and shrieked and said it was her kitty.

Daddy gave me a note from Mom, and I put it in my pocket to read later when there was some peace and quiet. Mrs. Hume had sent over a huge tuna fish and egg salad with bean sprouts, and two loaves of home-baked bread which pleased Daddy.

Dinner was not one of our happiest hours. Terry babbled on so much about the kitten that Daniel finally

told her to hush up, and Daddy told him not to be rude. The phone rang three times, and each time Andrew leaped up so fast he nearly tipped over his chair, as if we were going to fight him for the phone. I was trying to say that I washed my hands of the cat, and if Terry kept it, she could darned well take care of it, feed it, clean the litter box, and everything else.

Daniel was looking unhappy. Finally he said, "The kitten can have Mr. Quickly's scratching post until Q comes back, but then he'll have to give it up."

"She," I snapped at him. "The kitten is female."

Somewhere during the dessert, which was a Sara Lee cake, Daniel tried to pull himself together. "There's no reason why Terry shouldn't have a kitty," he said, as if he were giving her the keys to the kingdom. "Every child needs a pet."

Daddy waggled his eyebrows and got some more coffee. "Your mother will have to decide."

"It may be too late," I said, and then realized in the sudden silence how that sounded. "I mean if the cat stays one day, it'll be too late to take her back. She'll be part of the family." Now I was babbling, trying to erase what I'd just said.

"What are you going to name her, Terry?" Daniel said. He was making such an effort to sound cheerful, it was depressing.

"Kitty," Terry said.

I didn't want to talk about the darned cat any more. "Daniel got two A's in tests," I said.

He looked startled. "How'd you know?"

"Mr. Hergesheimer told me."

"That's wonderful, Dan," Daddy said.

"There goes our allowance," Andrew said. He winked at me. He was in that goofy revved-up state that always comes before a date.

"I'm proud of you," Daddy said. "Your mother will be pleased."

Daniel looked as if he felt better, really better, not just pretending.

"I'll take her to bed with me." Terry was still talking about the kitten.

"You can't call her Kitty," Andrew said. "If you call 'here, kitty, kitty,' what you'll get will be your sister." He guffawed as if he'd said something really witty.

"I've always favored Magnifi*cat* myself," Daddy said.

"Kitty," Terry said.

"How about *Cat*astrophe?" Andrew was really knocking himself out. I felt sorry for his date.

"How old is Kitty?" Terry demanded.

"Seven weeks," I said.

"I mean how old is she in real life?" she said, as if I were stupid or something.

"In human years," Daniel said, "she'd be in kindergarten."

That satisfied Terry, and no one questioned Daniel's logic.

I was sick of the kitten. I couldn't wait for dinner to be over so I could escape.

"Who wants an ice cream cone at the DQ?" Daddy said. "I have half an hour before visiting hours."

"Me!" Terry screamed.

"Me," Daniel said.

"I have to run." Andrew squirmed out of his chair.

"Be back by eleven," Daddy called after him, remembering to be parental. "How about you, Kit?"

"I have to water Mom's lilacs." I heard myself sound sulky.

He gave me a quick look. "It's going to rain."

"I can't count on it."

He said, "Have it your way."

And at last they were gone. I stacked the dishes; it was Daniel's turn to wash. I put on Mom's garden hat and got the kitten and went out back. The hat slid down to my eyebrows. I felt like a toadstool.

I got the hose and began to water the lilacs. They were budding. Mom dotes on lilacs. She planted bushes three times and they all got winter-killed, but these look okay.

The kitten was chasing imaginary dragons, leaping and whirling. I wanted to smile and enjoy her, but I felt sore inside.

Thunder sounded, far away, and the sky got a little darker, but I kept on watering. You couldn't ever be sure the storm would hit us.

I looked at one branch of lilacs that were almost

ready to burst into bloom, and suddenly it struck me that Mom might not be here when it bloomed. I felt as if I'd been struck by lightning. My body jerked and I went all stiff, with my arm stuck out holding the hose over the bush. Then I threw the hose down and sprawled on the grass and cried and cried.

Finally I stopped because the water from the hose was making puddles around my feet, and the kitten was chewing my hair. I sat up. The kitten jumped onto my chest and hung onto my T-shirt, staring at me. Her eyes were more violet than blue, like a pansy. "Pansy?" I said to her. "That's a goofy name." She looked deep into my eyes, not blinking. Maybe cats never blink. I hadn't noticed.

Her claws were digging in, so I put her down, and she did a wild dance after a white butterfly. When she caught it and killed it, it lay on the ground, stone-still. The kitten wanted to play with it, but I moved her away. I couldn't believe how unalive the butterfly looked, like a torn piece of paper. I held it in my hand, trying to think what it could mean, to be alive one second, and not alive the next. It really scared me.

I had to do something. I got the hoe from the garage and began to dig up some old cactus plants that grew beside the garage. Mom hated them. Somebody— Aunt Geraldine?—had planted them long ago. I chopped at them, hacking and hacking as hard as I could, till they lay in pieces all over the ground. When

I finished, I was breathing hard, and I had a blister on my hand.

All of a sudden there was a big clap of thunder, and it began to rain hard.

"Come on, Lilac," I said. I grabbed the kitten and ran for the house.

Chapter Thirteen

I WAS TRYING to think about anything except that today Miss Hortense Perry was going to say who won Best Author. I was pretty sure it would be me, and all my friends said so, but I wasn't *absolutely* sure.

I thought about the note Mom had sent me. It said, "Dearest Kit: I was sitting here thinking how odd it is that nowadays most girls' names are diminutives. Like Joni and Peggy and our Terry and Betsy and Sally. I wonder what that says about us. You were never called Kitty though, or Katie. Is that because you have such a strong personality? When the nurse came in, I was laughing like a maniac (I'm sure she thinks I'm pixilated anyway) because I was thinking of old book titles made diminutive, like *Annie of Green Gables*, and *Josie's Girls*, and *Buster Brown and His Sister Susie*, or how about *Romeo and Julie?* I tried to explain to the nurse why I was laughing, but she didn't get it. I thought, Kit will get it. Darling, I have all my fingers and my eyes crossed for your author adventure with the visiting poet. And you know you and I have a special bond, so maybe it will work. No, it won't take my wishing to make it true—it will come true because you are so gifted and so good. I love you with all my heart. Mom."

The note made me laugh, and it also made me cry. It was true Mom and I had always talked about the special tie between us. Maybe because we were both women. Terry was too little to be in on that, but she had other kinds of bonds with Mom. In fact, when I thought about it, I realized that each of us had. Oh, Mom, don't die!

"AND NOW, BOYS AND GIRLS," Mrs. Ramer said, beaming at us, "Miss Perry will announce her decision on your contributions."

Miss Perry stood up, knocking a paperclip off the desk. She seemed to be all over the place even when she was standing still.

"I won't prolong the agony," she said. "I want to say that there were some very, very good papers here, and I really had to read them several times before I made my decision." She gulped in air. "First place goes to . . ."

Anna poked me in the back. My heart was beating like a gong. I was afraid people could hear it.

". . . to Chu Vang!"

There was a moment of total silence. Everybody looked at me. I heard my heart break. Then one of the boys began to clap, and they all joined in. I remembered to clap, too. Mrs. Ramer was looking astonished.

I turned around and congratulated Chu. He looked very pleased, and for a second I had a mental picture of him as a little boy in a faraway land where his mother had her babies without a doctor and everything was cooked on a tiny charcoal stove. He had written a theme about it.

Then Anna was saying to me, "It's a gyp. You're the best."

And suddenly I felt very angry.

Miss Perry said, "And second place goes to . . . Katharine Esterly!"

My friends cheered and stomped. Mrs. Ramer had to wave her arms and look fierce to get order.

"Now, boys and girls, settle down. I'm sure we are all proud of Chu and Katharine, and we thank Miss Perry for her professional care and wisdom."

What a traitor!

"At three today she will meet with you, Chu, and Thursday at three with Katharine. And every day in class time she will give us a talk, which will make authors of us all, or at least better readers." Mrs. Ramer was rattled.

She tried to say something comforting to me after

class, but I pushed by her. I didn't wait for Daniel after school. Anna caught up with me and said, "It isn't fair."

"Oh, forget it," I said. "Who cares? She's just a kook. She gets published in magazines that don't pay anything, anyway."

"Except *The New Yorker*."

Some friend!

I tried to escape, but Anna followed me home. "Listen, I'll come over after supper. Let's cruise."

I didn't say yes, I didn't say no. What I said was, "I have to go in now. I have to fix dinner." It was only three o'clock, and Daddy had said he'd bring home Kentucky fried, but I wanted to let Anna know I was abused.

The first thing that happened was Andrew showed me the newspaper. There was the Children's Page, which comes out once a week. "How much do we owe him for this?" he said.

"This" was a poem by Daniel Esterly, Grade Three. The poem was:

What if a cow could talk?
What if a fish could walk?
What if the moon fell down?
What if a monster came to town?
What if cherry trees bore bread?
What if the sky was red?
What if a bird couldn't fly?
What if nothing could ever die?

Well, you would think Daniel had been appointed poet laureate. Such a to-do. Daddy had already taken a copy of the paper to Mom, and she called up to congratulate Daniel. I was proud of Daniel too, and I told him so; but I felt as if somebody had just taken the world away from me. Miss Hortense Perry, that's who it was.

Mom asked to talk to me. It was the first time she had called home, because the doctors had been trying to keep her very quiet and relaxed, but this time she insisted.

"Kit," she said, "how did it go with the Poet?"

"It bombed."

She didn't say anything for a couple of seconds. "I'm sorry. I think the Poet has made a mistake."

"Oh, I guess not," I said, sounding false and airy. "Chu Vang got it, and he's very good."

"Kit," she said, "did you know that when Beethoven wrote the Emperor Concerto, nobody would even play it?"

"I didn't know that." I was thinking my name isn't Beethoven.

"Nobody published *Billy Budd* until Melville was dead."

"Well, I hope his ghost threw a party."

"I wish I were home!" She sounded impatient, as if she were saying it to herself.

"Me, too." I was chewing the inside of my cheek to keep from bawling.

"I love you, and I believe in you. And I am not stupid. I know good writing when I see it. Let me speak to your father, before they make me hang up."

Daddy listened very carefully to whatever she said, and he looked at me a few times. I knew she was telling him about my failure. He didn't say anything to me about it, but he was unusually gentle with me, and at dinner when Andrew toasted Daniel with his glass of milk, Daddy said, "Now we have two writing talents in our family." He lifted his glass. "Here's to Daniel and here's to Katharine . . ."

I jumped up from the table and ran out of the room. I heard Terry say, "She wasn't excused." And I heard Daddy push back his chair. I tore out of the house and down the street toward Anna's house.

She was just coming out. "I have to go to the store for my mother. Hey, what's wrong? You look mad."

"Not mad. Just seeing the whole revolting world in its true light."

"Oh, you're still upset about that stupid poet. Listen, what does she know?" Anna is an athlete. She's on the field hockey team and the baseball team. She's A-number-one in gym. Everybody says we're an odd couple, but we get along fine. We aren't the kind of friends that tell each other everything. We more like relax with each other. No demands. I don't understand her, she doesn't understand me, and neither of us cares.

She is more reckless and adventurous than I am, but tonight I felt up to anything she wanted to suggest.

So when we came out of the Little Store, this little neighborhood grocery where you can buy stuff you forgot to get at the supermarket, she was carrying two dozen eggs, a loaf of bread, and a quart of two percent milk.

"I wish it were Hallowe'en," she said.

"Why?"

"I feel like making people mad."

"Me, too." I was interested. "Like how?"

We moseyed along a residential street where some of the more affluent people live. Some of the houses were nice, some were ugly-pretentious, some had no imagination. It was getting dark, and I knew I ought to go home. Daddy was going to the hospital and Andrew probably had a date, and I ought to be there with the little kids. But I didn't go.

"That's where Alison Marcus lives." Anna nodded toward a big brick house with a huge lion's head for a door knocker. There was a tennis court at one side. "Her old man owns the Oldsmobile-Mercedes dealership."

Alison Marcus was in the seventh grade, but she was a terrific athlete and sort of Anna's rival.

There were lights on all over the house.

"They must have a horrible electric bill," I said.

Anna had a thoughtful look that I recognized. It meant she was plotting. She opened one of the cartons of eggs, took out an egg and hefted it like a baseball.

I gasped. "Annie, you wouldn't!"

She grinned. She has a wide mouth, and when she smiles, it makes you feel kind of excited and ready for anything. "I wouldn't, huh?" She pulled her arm back and threw. Bull's-eye, right on the lion's head knocker. There was still enough light so we could see the yolk slowly dripping down the immaculate white door. It was very satisfying.

We walked away kind of fast. The egg had made just a very small plop sound. Probably nobody heard it. I almost wished they *had* heard it. It's not too much fun annoying people if they don't know they're being annoyed.

We came to a cutesy kind of house, painted robin's-egg blue with pale yellow shutters. It had a metal pixie on the grass and lots of flower beds. "Whoever lives there," I said, "is twee."

Anna took out another egg. "One runny yoke for the house that is a joke." Plop. The egg hit a yellow shutter. There's one thing about Anna, she's right on target.

My arm was twitching, I wanted so much to throw an egg. I didn't care at who or at what. Just to make that lovely sickening plop in the eye of the world. I took an egg out of the carton. It felt cold and wonderful in my sweaty hand. I hurled it with all my strength across the street at a house that sat close to the sidewalk. I was aiming at the porch light, an elaborate wrought iron thing that wasn't on. Probably a million-dollar lamp with a burned-out bulb.

I don't have Anna's eye. The egg hit a window. In a couple of seconds the porch light went on. We ran.

Nothing could stop us now. We spattered doors, cars (especially clean ones), front steps, mailboxes. At one house we broke an egg inside a mailbox, so whoever went for the mail would put his hand in all that goo. It was wonderful. I felt liberated.

A car came out of a side street right in front of me as I had my arm drawn back to throw. I knew it was a mistake but the temptation was too much: I hit the window on the driver's side.

The car braked to a quick stop. We ran. Somebody was yelling, and he sounded mad. We darted up a dead-end street, discovered our mistake, ran back and found another side street and wove in and out of streets throwing eggs as we ran. A kid on a bike caught one right on the chest. He bellowed. We ran. It was like a TV chase scene.

We had only two eggs left when we came to a stop near the River School, and suddenly I thought of Anna Wong crossing the river. For just a second I felt as if she was telling me to cut it out, to go home and act serious. I talked back to her in my mind. I knew we were acting like crazy little kids. But a person can only take so much. Then she has to burst out and get it off her chest. We were making a mess, but we weren't smashing anything. It was the missile, not the target, that got broken.

We divided the last of the eggs. Anna aimed at the door of a great big Colonial reproduction. The door had fanlights above it, and they were her target. Wind up, aim, throw. Right on the nose! The egg slowly spread over the glass and oozed down onto the door.

"Beautiful!" I said. Down the street a way, a car came out of another street and stopped. In a few seconds the headlights went out. Somebody coming home late from work probably. I decided I'd like to throw my last egg at the headlight of the car. Get even with that other guy in a car who yelled at us.

I eased along the street, keeping in the shadows. Anna followed. I hadn't heard the car door open and close, so I slowed up a little. Then I heard it, *thunk, thunk*, and footsteps, and a shadowy outline of somebody going up the walk to a house. There wasn't any streetlight there, and I couldn't see the person.

I waited in the shadows till I was sure whoever it was had had time to go into the house. It was really dark, with huge trees hanging out over the sidewalk. I remember thinking it must be a lot of leaves to rake up in the fall.

I aimed at the pale round headlight on the sidewalk side. This guy had parked on the wrong side of the street. So he was a lawbreaker, too. I pulled my arm back and gripped the egg.

Anna had come up right behind me, and all of a sudden she whispered, "Wait!" But I was too concentrated to pay any attention. I threw the egg as hard as I could, and just as it hit the headlight, a perfect shot, I registered that those shadows on top of the car weren't ski racks. They were lights. It was a police car!

Chapter
Fourteen

"... AND WE GOT A COUPLE OF COMPLAINTS, SO I came out to take a look." The policeman, the biggest one I've ever seen, had Anna by one arm and me by the other. He was telling Anna's mother what we had done.

She kept looking at me as if she could believe it of Anna, but she couldn't believe I'd done anything so wicked. "I'm sorry," she said. "I can't imagine . . . We'll pay to clean up whatever needs cleaning up. We'll punish Anna, and I'm sure the Esterlys will do the same." She hesitated. "Mrs. Esterly is in the hospital." She looked at me again as if something had dawned on her. "That may be why . . . It's quite serious, Mrs. Esterly's condition. Perhaps you could go a little easy?"

The policeman had an unreadable face. I couldn't tell if he was going to put us in jail or not. I sort of thought he was. All the family faces flashed through my mind. I could see each one of them visiting me in jail. I could imagine my mother getting a terrible headache because of her daughter's criminal behavior. I saw my father resigning in disgrace. Andrew would run away from home because he couldn't stand the shame. Daniel and Terry would be bullied at school. I wished I could die.

"Well, ma'am," the officer was saying, "I'll have to make out a report. We'll put your daughter in your jurisdiction for thirty days. At that time you and she will come to the station house and report. If she's kept out of trouble, we'll drop the charges." He scowled at Anna. "It's up to you, young lady."

"Yes sir," Anna whispered. It was the only time I've ever seen her cowed.

He marched me back to the police car. I hesitated, not knowing whether I was to get in back or in front. I thought he would probably handcuff me. "Get into the vee-hick-el," he said, opening the front door. I got in.

As he drove toward my house, he talked on his intercom thing. ". . . on Harris Avenue, west of Alder. Apprehended two juveniles throwing eggs at houses. One suspect threw an egg at the headlamp of the p'lice car. Left first suspect with her mother. Now proceeding to second suspect's house. Over and out." He speeded up, and I thought he was going to turn on the siren, but he didn't.

Second suspect. He was talking about me. Katharine Esterly, second suspect. I couldn't even be first in crime.

I tried to imagine my father's face when he opened the door and saw me being accompanied by an arresting officer. I couldn't imagine it.

But Daddy was not home. Not back from the hospital. It was Daniel who opened the door. His face would have been funny if it hadn't been such a terrible situation. He looked as if the world had suddenly spun off its axis right before his eyes. I could hear Andrew's stereo playing punk rock. How appropriate.

"Your dad home, son?" the p'lice officer said.

Daniel shook his head.

"Expecting him soon?"

Daniel gulped. He was incapable of speech.

I said, "He's at the hospital to see my mother."

"I see." The policeman lapsed into deep thought. Then he got a pad and a ballpoint pen from his pocket. He wrote down a phone number and his name. "Ask him to call me, please." He held it out to Daniel.

Daniel just looked at him. Then he put out his hand and took the paper, still staring at the policeman as if he were hypnotized.

Heart of Stone softened a little. "That's all right, son," he said. He let go of my arm and left.

I stepped into the hall and closed the door. Andrew was on the stairs. He was staring at me, too. "Was that the fuzz?" he said.

"Obviously," I snapped.

"What did he want?"

"Me. I'm a dangerous criminal." I burst into tears and ran upstairs.

Quite a while later Daddy knocked on my door. I braced myself. It didn't seem fair, all this fuss over a few eggs when other people were destroying property and starting fires and mugging helpless victims. I was all ready to say that, but I didn't get the chance.

He sat down on the bed and took my hand. "Your mother is going to be operated on in the morning."

"Oh, Daddy!" I forgot all about eggs.

He held me for a few minutes. "Pray hard, Kit. Think positive thoughts. We'll get her through this together."

After he had gone, I lay on my stomach gripping the pillow so hard my hands ached. I felt somehow as if I had brought it on, being so lawless. I knew that didn't make sense, but I couldn't get it out of my head. I was awake almost all night, praying and gritting my teeth and ESPing the surgeon to get it right. Don't hurt my mother! If she comes out all right, I promise I'll turn myself into something she'll be proud of. I don't know what, but I'll find something. I promise!

Chapter
Fifteen

I woke up with the sun shining on my face and the kitten, Lilac, asleep in the crook of my knees. Lilac had settled into the family, but Daniel was as polite and distant to her as if she were a visiting aunt.

I thought it was Saturday, but suddenly I came to. It was a school day. The clock alarm was shut off, and the hands said twenty to ten. Why hadn't somebody awakened me? Then everything came flooding back. My criminal behavior. The police. Mom's operation.

Why hadn't I asked Daddy what time the operation would be? Maybe it was over. I was scared to think about it, but I couldn't stop. If she had died, I would know it. I would feel it. I was sure I would.

The house was deathly still. I felt as if I were the only person left in the world.

I opened my door, and Lamb fell against my feet.

Daniel had left him to comfort me. I was so touched, I was afraid I was going to start crying again, and if I did, I might never stop.

The thing to do was to act as if it were a normal day. I took a shower and brushed my teeth and went downstairs, clutching Lamb. He is kind of dingy from much living and much washing, but he felt soft and comforting. I was glad Daniel had left him.

In the kitchen there was a note for me from Andrew. That was surprising. It said, "Dear Sis- Cheer up. Andrew." Why was everybody being so nice to me? Maybe they knew something I didn't know. Maybe the policeman had decided to put me in jail after all. Did they have a special jail for kids? I wished I could check with Anna, but she'd be in school. Why had Daddy let me oversleep and miss school?

Maybe something terrible had happened to Mom. I got the phone book. My fingers were shaking so much, I could hardly find the hospital's number.

When the hospital person answered, I said, "I'm Katharine Esterly. My mother is being operated on. I want to find out if she's all right."

"One moment please."

I had to say it all over again to somebody else. My voice sounded squeaky.

"Mrs. Esterly is resting comfortably."

She sounded as if she was going to hang up. "Wait. Has she had the operation?"

"Yes, she has."

"She didn't . . . she didn't die or anything?"

"Oh, no."

"But is she going to be all right?"

"I'm sorry, I can't tell you that. She is resting comfortably."

I hung up. It was over, and she was alive. That was something to hang onto. But she could be brain damaged . . . That wasn't thinkable. Not my mother. Not that bright, funny, loving brain.

I didn't know what to do. I drank some grapefruit juice and thought about cereal, but I couldn't face eating. I went upstairs and went back to bed with Lamb.

Half an hour later I heard Daddy's car. I was scared to hear what he had to say, so I stayed where I was. Pretty soon he came upstairs. I tried to tell from the sound of his footsteps whether he was sad or happy or what. I couldn't tell.

And I couldn't tell from his face. He looked serious. I tried to ask him and couldn't get the words out.

He sat down on the bed. "Well, it's over, Kit."

"How . . . how did it . . . ?"

"She made it. They got the tumor out. They can't tell yet for sure, but it looks promising. She was just coming out of the anesthetic when I left."

"They can't tell for sure what?"

"Whether she . . ." A look of pain crossed his face. He looked terribly tired. "Whether it's benign. They're pretty sure it is. If not, it could recur, but Dr. Bernard says they'll be watching her, and if it does, they can catch it early."

I felt angry. Why couldn't they make up their minds whether she was all right or not all right?

"Do you want to come down and have some breakfast with me?"

I was still in my bathrobe, but I went down with him. He made toast and coffee and some cocoa for me. He was wearing jeans and an old sweat shirt. I knew he must have cancelled his classes for the day.

Stirring his coffee he said, "About this police business."

I gritted my teeth.

"I was really startled. I mean you're the level-headed one. I understand you've been under a strain. We all have. But we can't take it out on innocent people, can we."

I shook my head and stared into the cocoa. It was getting a thin skim on top. I hate that. I spooned it off.

"I'll have to ground you for three weeks. And you're . . . uh . . . in my custody for a month. Then I have to report to the police that you have not committed any . . . er . . . misdemeanors."

I looked up and for a second I thought there was a smile in his eyes, but that didn't seem likely.

"Officer Riley gave me a list of the people who complained." He fished around in his jeans pocket and brought out a piece of paper. "I think it would be a good idea if you wrote them each a note of apology."

"All right." There were five names on the list. Five complaints out of two dozen eggs. We were lucky. I hate apologizing for anything. It would be awful to have to do it twenty-four times.

He looked at his watch. "I'm going back to the hospital. Will you look after Terry when she gets home? I told Mrs. Hume you were here, so she won't need to come over."

"All right."

He stood up and stretched. "It's been a terrible strain, hasn't it. I *think* we're in the clear, but keep hoping. As soon as I know anything more, I'll call you."

I decided I'd better get the apologies over with. It might keep me from thinking too much. I went up to my room and worked out a letter on my scratch pad. "Dear Whoever: I am very sorry about the egg mess. It was a wrong thing to do. I hope it did not damage your property. Yours sincerely, Katharine Esterly."

I had actually written four of them before I realized that I was using my bird stationery. I screamed, balled them up and threw them in the waste paper basket, and went back to bed with Lamb.

Chapter
Sixteen

It was Thursday night before we really knew about Mom.

"She's going to be all right," Daddy said at dinner. "She's going to be all right, kids!" He looked ten years younger, and he had made himself a bourbon on the rocks. "It was benign."

"What's that?" Daniel said.

"Not malignant, not evil, not a cancer. When it's gone, it's gone. Her reactions are fine. It was a neuro-fibromas tumor, which means a tumor of the brain nerves, as I understand it."

"When's Mommy coming home?" Terry said.

"In about two weeks."

"I want her to come now."

"Hush up, Terry," Andrew said. "Dad, did they shave her head?"

"They did, yes. That's routine."

"Shave her head!" Daniel looked appalled.

I knew how he felt. Our mother without all her beautiful hair? It was painful to imagine.

"That's nothing," Andrew said. "It'll grow back. I did a paper on brain tumors for science. I read all about it. They take a little saw and drill holes in the skull and lift out a block of bone and . . ."

I ran as fast as I could to the downstairs bathroom and threw up. How could she possibly be all right if they had done such terrible things? My own head ached and pounded.

Daddy washed my face as if I were some kind of baby, and he took me upstairs. "All that is over," he said. "She's doing fine, Kit. I wouldn't lie to you."

"How can she be all right with part of her head gone?"

"No, no, it's not gone. They put it back. It's very neatly stitched back."

"She'll be all scarred."

"I promise you, she won't. There'll be a very fine scar underneath her hair."

"She hasn't got any hair."

"Kit!" He was beginning to sound impatient. "She *will* have."

I couldn't accept it.

"Listen," Daddy said, "I was thinking. When your mother comes home, why don't we have a little celebration? Walter suggested it. He's offered to do the honors. It will be a quiet party, because your mother will still be feeling weak, but think about it. Think of some nice things to do." He kissed me and left.

I couldn't think about it. All I could think of was that she was not going to be the same mother. She was going to have a totally bald head like Yul Brynner or Telly Savalas. With a horrible scar. What if they fitted the bone section back crooked?

ON FRIDAY MORNING I had a second conference with Miss Perry. She had had classes with us and with the other grades. Even Daniel's class had her, and she told him how much she liked his poem. Daniel was getting A's right and left, just because he was bothering to do his homework. Andrew and I were going broke.

At my first conference, on Thursday, Miss Perry had told me that although I wrote "nicely," my story didn't ring true because I was writing about a character and a situation that were not familiar to me. I wanted to say that Shakespeare had never been in Denmark, but that didn't stop him from writing *Hamlet*. Only of course I didn't say it. I was still too upset to listen very much to what she was saying. I didn't know why, if I was so terrible, she would want a second conference.

On Thursday we had had to write a paper on a poem from a bunch of Xeroxed sheets that she gave us. There were three poems by her and half a dozen by other poets. I guess she hoped we would all choose one of hers, but I picked "Douglas Fir" by Myra Cohn Livingston. It begins *"Tall*

> *shaggy*
>
> *curmudgeon*
>
> *rugged*
>
> *forester*
>
> *with furrowed*
>
> *bark,"*

and it reminded me of a particular fir tree in the Chinese graveyard that I really like. It's a curmudgeon, too. And I liked the odd way the poem was arranged. It almost looked like a tree.

So on Friday I was expecting Miss Perry to frown at me for not choosing her poem, but instead she gave me this big shiny smile, and she said, "Katharine, your paper was delightful. It was really perceptive."

I gulped and thanked her.

"You have a real ear."

I wanted to say I had two of 'em, but that would be sassy. So I muttered thank you again.

"Mrs. Ramer gave me this . . ." She had some papers spread out on the desk. I looked and got a real shock. It was my old story about the garter snake.

"Why did she give you that old thing?"

"Because she thought, and I am inclined to agree, that 'that old thing' is a better example of your talent than the Chinese story. It is not as polished or as mature in style, of course, but it has a freshness and humor and charm that the other one lacks."

"The other one wasn't supposed to be funny."

"No, of course not." She paused and lit a cigarette.

I was kind of shocked. We kids aren't supposed to smoke, so what kind of an example was this? Besides, if she wasn't careful, she'd set all that hair on fire.

"I understand," she said, "that your mother has been very ill. Underwent serious surgery."

I nodded. What business was it of hers?

"I realize that you must have been under a great strain, and that is probably why you chose to write about another girl who also suffered over the illness of her mother."

"I guess so." I hadn't thought of it that way.

"Are you familiar with Wordsworth's remarks on recollection in tranquility?"

I said I wasn't. It really was risky, the way she gestured with that cigarette so close to her hair. What if the whole school burned down because of a poet's hair?

She took five or six minutes to tell me what Wordsworth meant. In a nutshell, he was saying if you write from your own emotional experiences, wait awhile till you cool down.

"Now what I want you to do, Katharine, is to rewrite your little garter snake story. Don't change it basically. Just give it the smoothness of your present-day style. Don't get self-conscious about it. Just let it flow."

"What for?"

She was beginning to lose patience with me. " 'What for?' Because it's so good. I want to submit this one to the paper rather than the other one. With your permission of course."

I was disgusted. Really! That dumb, childish old story! But I was afraid if I didn't do it, she wouldn't submit anything, and then I'd really feel humiliated.

So during lunch hour I rewrote it, gagging all the way. It seemed so childish! I didn't know whether it was worse not to be in the paper at all or to be in it with that dumb little fantasy. Well, as Mrs. Ramer likes to say, we shall see what we shall see.

Chapter
Seventeen

LATE THAT AFTERNOON, Miss Hortense Perry carried on about my rewritten story as if it was *The Hobbit* or something. I had retitled it, "The Garter Snake Caper." Not very original, but she loved it. I'm not sure about her taste. Or else she was trying to let me down easy for having lost to Chu.

At the end of a little "chat" at three o'clock, she said, "Katharine, I've spoken to Chu about this, and I think it would be nice if we changed the situation so that you and Chu are tied for first place. He agrees. I showed him the story, and he loved it."

"Oh, no," I said. "No. Chu won fair and square. I didn't even submit this story."

She peered into my face with her pale blue eyes. "Well, all right, Katharine. If that's how you want it."

"That's how I want it."

"Very well. That's very generous of you."

That made me mad. Of course it wasn't generous. I didn't want that dumb story getting first place. And it would be a rotten trick to play on Chu. Of course he agreed, because he's a nice kid, but it would spoil it for him. He has a huge family here, aunts and uncles and cousins and all, and think how proud they're going to be of him. I thought about it on the way home, and I almost began to be glad he'd won.

To my surprise, he called me on the phone, just after I got home, to say it was okay with him if we shared. "It's a neat story," he said.

"No," I said. "No way. I appreciate it, but you won first place, I didn't."

His voice sounded warm and relieved when he said, "Well, if you're sure that's how you want it."

"I'll bet your family are pleased," I said.

He laughed, actually laughed. "They're going to have a big party on publication day. Would you come? To the party?"

I was really touched. "I'd love to."

"Nobody knows when they'll publish our things, but my mother's already started cooking."

I laughed, too, then. "I guess that's how moms are."

I hung up thinking how glad I was to have a mom to share remarks about with Chu, and how glad I was

1 1 6

that he had his mom. I guess they had a very hard time getting out of Vietnam. He's never talked about it, but my father has one of Chu's cousins in his survey course.

Daddy was in the kitchen cutting Daniel's hair. We have a huge old-fashioned kitchen, and Daniel was sitting on one of the bar stools in the middle of the room. They were talking about the kind of boats the ancient Phoenicians used.

"They also invented the alphabet," Daddy said, "at least as far as western civilization was concerned."

Snip-snip-snip.

"I wonder what it was like without an alphabet," Daniel said.

I left them figuring that one out, and took *The Joy of Cooking* out onto the back steps. Since I was grounded anyway, I had decided I might as well cook some decent meals. I'd had a great success with brownies and I'd done a chicken the five-spice way, but yesterday I'd used the leftover chicken for something called Mexican chicken with rice, and it had been a dismal failure. The rice hadn't cooked right. Daddy had taken one mouthful and said, "Is this what they mean by biting the bullet?"

He took us to the Bar MG for the Lone Prairie special.

This time I wanted to come up with a decent meal. I decided on a spaghetti casserole with onions and pimientos and cream sauce, with grated cheddar and breadcrumbs on top. I sat awhile on the steps in the sunshine, thinking about Mom. She had to go through all this cooking bit every day, plus teaching. It was no cinch being a house-person. Unless maybe you were like Mrs. Hume, who didn't seem to want to do anything else. But maybe when Mrs. Hume was young and single, she'd dreamed of being . . . what? Maybe private secretary to a movie star. She'd like that. Or maybe she'd wanted to be a ballet dancer. That made me giggle.

In the kitchen Daniel and Daddy were cleaning up. Dan was shorn and clipped, like Marjorie Ainsworth's poodle. I thought about Mama's beautiful hair, all gone. But if I sat there thinking about that, I'd get too depressed to fix dinner. So I got up and went inside and began to make the sauce for the casserole.

Terry came barreling downstairs, and I heard Daniel say, "Where's your kitten?"

"Oh, she's up the pine tree, the big one. She ran up there before I took my nap. I told her and told her to come down, but she wouldn't."

Daniel sounded upset. "You shouldn't have a kitten. You don't even remember to feed her."

"I've been busy with Genevieve." Genevieve was a large, grotesque rag doll that Aunt Meg had sent her from somewhere in Europe.

Daniel's voice rose. "You stupid child! Lilac is *alive*. You can't just . . . Oh, never mind. What tree is she in?"

"Back of the garage." As he ran through the kitchen, she called after him. "You can have her if you want her."

Daniel muttered something fierce and ran out the back door, slamming it. In a minute he came back. "Kit, help me carry the ladder. Lilac's up a tree and scared to come down."

I started to say I couldn't leave my sauce just when it was beginning to thicken, but then I thought of his voice when he said, 'Lilac is *alive!*' And I went. First things first. That must be one of the basic lessons mothers have to learn.

Poor little Lilac was hunched up on the lowest limb of the pine. The branches on trees like that start high up. She certainly couldn't jump, and she was scared to back down the trunk. I remembered a couple of times when Q had gotten himself into the same fix. Kittens don't plan ahead.

Daniel scrambled up the ladder, talking to Lilac all the time. When he got her down, she curled up around his neck, the way Q used to. I saw the emotion in his face, and I had to look away.

"She likes you," I said.

"Terry's gotten bored with her. I guess I'll have to look after her. Somebody has to." He looked at me. "If it's okay with you." He was considering me to be in charge of the kitten because I'd brought it home.

"Sure," I said. I started to add that that had been the idea in the first place, but then decided that wasn't the right thing to say.

At that moment, Lilac became Daniel's cat. He continued to look for Q, and he tensed up when there was any cat in the neighborhood that looked at all like Q. But he loved Lilac, and she loved him. Some people are born to have cats.

Chapter Eighteen

MOM HAD BEEN TALKING to us every day on the phone. She wasn't supposed to talk long, so she took one child each day. It happened to be me the day she told us she was coming home.

"Tomorrow, Kit!" Her voice still sounded shaky and thin. Daddy said she had lost weight.

I was scared. "Are you sure you're ready?"

She laughed, not her usual strong throaty laugh, but a kind of shaky sound. "Am I ever! I can't wait. I miss you so."

I wanted more than anything to see her, but I was terrified. Would she be all right? Maybe she had changed. You couldn't have your brain messed with and not change. I felt as though I couldn't deal with it.

And she'd be bald. How would we be able to keep from staring at her Telly Savalas head? In my mind her face began to look like Telly Savalas, too. Still, when she got all right again (if she ever did), it would be wonderful not to have to cope. I was sick of cooking, sick of dealing with Terry's whining, which had gotten worse since Mom left. Sick of being the one Andrew had to talk to about his new girl. Although actually I liked her. She sang and played the dobro and the mandolin. She and Andrew had gotten a group together, hoping to get some gigs at school or wherever. Sometimes they practiced at our house, and they sounded good. Her name was Emma. She wasn't one of Mom's diminutives. I took that as a good sign.

I told the other kids what Mom had said about coming home. Terry shrieked with delight and ran off to tell her new doll. Thank goodness she had abandoned the Kanakeens. Daniel and Andrew both got a kind of cautious look, and I knew they felt the way I did.

"I'll call up Uncle Walt," Daniel said. "He's going to do the dinner."

"Maybe she'll be too sick," I said.

"Don't be silly," Andrew said, trying to sound confident. "She's coming *home* from the hospital. That means she's okay."

"Will she wear a wig?" Daniel said.

The telephone rang again, and Andrew leaped for it as usual. "For you." He held it out to me.

I thought it would be Anna. She's grounded too, so we talk a lot on the phone and complain about how unjustly persecuted we are. She reads me newspaper accounts of real vandalism and points out how ours was just a prank. My family doesn't talk to me about it, and personally I'd like to forget the whole thing, but I guess when you commit crimes and misdemeanors they haunt you for a long time. Mom had never mentioned it, and I didn't know if she knew about it or not.

It wasn't Anna. It was a woman who said she was an editor at the newspaper. She said, "We're planning to run your story in the weekend edition, in the *Entertainer* section, a week from Friday. I'd like to get some biographical detail from you, Katharine, and if you have a picture we could use, that'd be fine. If not, our photographer will come around and get a few shots, if that's okay with you."

I felt dazed. My *picture?* In the paper? "I . . . uh . . . I guess I have some." Daddy is a compulsive picture-taker of his kids.

"Wonderful." She asked a bunch of questions, when was I born, where, number of siblings, what exactly did Daddy teach . . . That one boggled my mind; she knew more about me than she did about Daddy. What kind of writer did I plan to be? Novels, short stories, poems?

"All of the above," I said, and she laughed. She sounded young and businesslike.

What were my hobbies? Hobbies? I couldn't think. I had a wild impulse to say egg-throwing. "Reading," I said. "Cooking sometimes. If I don't have to. Walking in the woods. Latin."

"*Latin?*"

I felt apologetic. It did sound goofy. "I mean I like Latin a lot, and I usually do more than my homework."

"That's interesting," she said. "Fascinating. Well, I guess that covers it."

I was about to hang up when she said, "Katharine?"

"Yes?"

"I really love your story. All of us here are charmed by it."

"You are?" I couldn't believe it.

"You write with great humor and style and panache."

I gulped and managed to say thank you. She thanked me and hung up. Panache. *Panache?* I went into Daddy's study and looked it up. An ornamental plume worn on a helmet. What! I must have misunderstood her.

"Who was that?" Andrew said.

"The newspaper. I was being interviewed."

Andrew's eyes blinked. "No kidding. What for? I hope it wasn't about the . . . you know . . . eggs?"

"Of course not. It was about my story. I'm being published next week Friday."

"Wow! That's wonderful."

"My picture will be in the paper. Maybe on the cover of the *Entertainer*." I was making that part up. She hadn't said anything about the cover. But it *could* happen.

"Chu Vang, too?" Daniel said.

I'd forgotten about Chu. Now his mother could really get cracking. And I'd be going to his party.

"One of Daddy's graduate students is going to interview me," Daniel said.

"Why?" Andrew said.

"He's doing a paper on gifted children."

Andrew groaned. "What am I doing in this family?"

"You'll be in the paper, too," I said, to comfort him. "When people hear your group play. You really sound great, Andrew."

He grinned. "Emma's terrific, isn't she?"

"So are you." I wanted everybody to feel good. I felt good. I went upstairs whistling.

Chapter Nineteen

SHE WAS HOME! I hadn't seen her yet because she came while we were still in school, and she was resting. I was so nervous, I was shaking. I wanted to tear upstairs and look, and I was too scared to go anywhere near her. She was bound to be different. I braced myself.

Daddy and Uncle Walt were in the kitchen, and Daddy couldn't stop grinning. Uncle Walt was roasting a goose, "in lieu of the fatted calf," he said. The kitchen smelled so good, it was absolutely dizzy-making. If the government ever takes away Uncle Walt's Social Security and his Air Force pension, he could make a fortune as a cook.

He waved a big wooden spoon at me. "I brought you a present, Katharine." He pointed to a book on the table. "One author to another."

I opened it. It was an old book, copyrighted 1951.

It was full of photographs with captions. There was General Joe Stilwell. And Chiang Kai Shek and Madame Chiang Kai Shek at Wellesley College, the caption said. Views of China and Burma. Pictures of tattered-looking soldiers. I flipped back to the title page. "Photographs by Walter E. Dodge." I was really impressed. Daddy had said that Uncle Walt used to take pictures all over the world, but I didn't know he was *published*. I felt awed.

"I didn't know you had a book. I thought you just took snapshots, home movies and stuff."

He laughed. "I took plenty of snapshots all right."

"He used to sell his pictures to *Life* magazine," Daddy said.

"He never told us."

Daniel came into the kitchen with Lilac hung around his neck. Which reminded me, the lilacs were in bloom. I gave Uncle Walt a hug and went outside to cut some lilac branches for the big copper vase. I felt tingly.

The smell of the lilacs was enough to knock you over. I wondered if it would be too strong for Mom. She usually loved it, but now that she wasn't very well . . . I stood there in indecision. I hate indecision. I cut off two sprays. It had rained in the night, and little showers of raindrops fell off the lilac bush onto my hands and arms. It felt cool and nice.

I thought about Uncle Walt, famous, and I hadn't known it. I hadn't ever really thought about what he used to be except in war. If I was going to be a writer, I'd have to learn to think about people more. Charm. The newspaper office was charmed. I pictured them all sitting in a circle reading my story over and over and looking at each other in amazement that a twelve-year-old girl could write such a charming story. Hogwash! She probably just said that to be polite. Still, she had sounded as if she really liked it. Amazing. That silly little story! Maybe writers never knew when they were good and when they weren't. Poor Anna Wong, hung up out there in the middle of the river. I was beginning to see, though, that maybe she sounded too modern, too much like me in the way she thought.

I looked up at Mom's bedroom window and wished I could look at her first from a distance, kind of get used to her.

Emma was coming to dinner. I didn't mind at all. In fact, I was glad. Only I hated to have her meet our mother for the first time when Mama was bald. What would she think? I hoped Andrew had explained.

When I went in, Uncle Walt said, "Katharine, you've kept this kitchen in apple-pie order. Everything neat as a pin."

"She's been wonderful," Daddy said. "She's held this family together."

I couldn't believe he said that. I didn't know he had even noticed. He must have forgotten about the eggs.

"Your mother asked me to wake her at five." He looked at his watch. "Do you want to come with me?"

I panicked. "No," I said, "no, I'd better wait till she comes down. I mean I don't want to upset her . . ."

He looked puzzled. "She won't be upset. She's so happy to be home, and she can't wait to see you."

Uncle Walt saved me. "If you don't mind, Katharine, I need help in setting the table. You know where everything is."

I practically fell into the drawer where we keep the tablecloth and napkins. Daddy went upstairs alone.

Uncle Walt looked at me. He was finishing a bowl of extra stuffing, with sliced chestnuts and stuffed olives and a little white wine. "It's all right, Kit," he said, "everything's fine."

My hands shook so much, I dropped Andrew's napkin ring. I was thinking of a dream I'd had, that Mom had really died and the person who was coming home from the hospital was a stranger.

Chapter
Twenty

WHEN MOM CAME DOWNSTAIRS, I felt as if I should make a deep curtsey, the way the English do for their queen. As if this was somebody special and apart from us mortals, someone I felt as if I knew but really didn't. That's a weird way to feel about your own mother. I was shaking. If I really had had to curtsey, I'd probably have fallen over.

She looked different but very beautiful and exotic. She was wearing a gold-colored cap that fitted close to her head like a helmet, and the housecoat Daddy gave her last Christmas that's more like a gown to wear to a party. It's gold-colored too, and slinky. She hasn't worn it very often before, because she said it was so elegant, she had to feel up to it. I guess she felt up to it now.

All of us kids stood around staring at her. She

hugged each one of us, and then she leaned back against Daddy's arm and looked at us as if she couldn't look at us hard enough. Finally she laughed. "Don't look so awed. It's only me."

Terry burst into wails, and Mom had to hug her again and tell her everything was all right. Then Terry wanted to poke under Mom's cap, and Daddy had to haul her off. Really, that child can be impossible.

After that, we all got terribly busy, helping Uncle Walt and running around and bumping into each other. Andrew came with Emma, and the two of them sat with Mom in the living room. Daddy was one big walking grin. He couldn't stay away from Mom.

Uncle Walt was smiling and humming while he and we got the dinner on the table. I tried to relax and enjoy it, but I couldn't. All through dinner, I kept looking sideways at Mom to see if she was really the same person. She looked pale and thinner and kind of tired, and she sort of sat back and let other people do things, which was unusual, but she didn't seem different otherwise. At least I kept telling myself she didn't. No brain damage.

Everybody was terribly nice to everybody else. Andrew told Mom and Emma about all the A's Daniel was getting, and Daniel told them how my story and my picture were going to be in the paper, and I talked about how wonderful Andrew's and Emma's music was. Daddy just beamed at us all, and Uncle Walt made sure we all had enough of everything. It was a great dinner, only I kept forgetting to pay attention to it. Daddy made a fuss over the bread I had baked the day before, and Mom was impressed. It was the first time I had ever made bread. It's quite an interesting process, actually.

After dinner things got better. We went out on the patio, which is on the side of the house that faces the garden. Mom was thrilled about the lilacs. She sat in the old chaise longue, and we all clustered around her, like petals from the center of a flower. Except of course nobody was behind her. Uncle Walt brought espresso coffee for the grownups (which included Andrew and Emma) and cinnamon tea for us kids. I began to relax.

"Somebody chopped down those awful cacti," Mom said.

"I did."

"Oh, thank God. Every time I started to do it, I felt Aunt Geraldine's presence saying, 'Dorothy, what *do* you think you're doing!'"

"She didn't bother me," I said, and everybody laughed. I was sitting on a leather hassock close to Mom's knees. She put out her hand and stroked my hair. "I think we should consider getting your hair cut."

"Really?" I couldn't believe it. I've been wanting to get it cut for so long.

"Oh, no," Daddy groaned.

"Oh yes," Mom said firmly. "She's going to high school in the fall. She can't go in braids."

The doorbell rang, and Daniel jumped up. "It's

for me," he said. He made an airy gesture. "My interviewer."

Daddy explained to Emma about his student interviewing Daniel. "I seem to have gotten him into this."

"He'll enjoy it," Andrew said. "And the interviewer will go away with a headache, wondering how he could have such terrible gaps in his education. In the interviewer's education, I mean."

Emma was holding Terry in her lap. "You have very special children, Mrs. Esterly," she said. She meant it.

"I know," Mom said. "I know." She was wearing dark glasses, even though it was almost dark out. She leaned toward me. "You're ungrounded as of tonight."

I was startled. I didn't know she knew about all that. I wished she hadn't brought it up.

Andrew had heard her. "That was quite an eggsperience Kit had," he said in his most innocent voice.

"Quite beyond our eggspectations," Mom said.

Maybe I was imagining that they were saying *eggs* instead of *ex.* I thought Mom's mouth twitched, but how could she be smiling.

"An eggspert, from all I've heard," Daddy said.

I was blushing all over. How could they laugh at such a thing? Or were they laughing? I leaned against Mom's knees and whispered, "Please take your glasses off, just for a minute."

She took them off. Her eyes were laughing. Loving

laughter. She didn't think I was a criminal! She still loved me. And she really *was* the same mother. You couldn't mistake that look in her eyes.

She leaned forward and hugged me tight. "But once is enough."

"I know," I said. "Oh, I know."

Uncle Walt brought out his harmonica, and Andrew went to get his guitar and Emma's dobro. Daddy walked by the living room and came back to say that Daniel was looking a bit beleaguered.

Mom said, "Kit, why don't you go and give him moral support."

"The interviewer won't like it."

"A pox on the interviewer," Daddy said. "He's only a graduate student." He likes to put down his students, but he doesn't mean it.

Uncle Walt was playing softly as I went into the house. In a minute Andrew and then Emma joined in. They were playing "Shenandoah."

The interviewer was tall and skinny, bearded and bespectacled, dressed in jeans with a worn patch on the knee and a faded green T-shirt that said VIRGINIA WOOLF. I thought he looked a little desperate. Daniel shot me a look that plainly said: Get me out of here.

I sat down at the back of the room and pretended I was looking for a book in the wall bookcase. I picked one at random and faked great interest. It was one of the Harvard Classics, *Plato, Epictetus, Marcus Aurelius.* I opened it to Epictetus, and I really got interested in what he was saying. "Give thyself more diligently to reflection: Know thyself: take counsel with the Godhead: without God put thine hand unto nothing!" I flipped the page. "No man can rob us of our Will—no man can lord over that!" I wondered if Epictetus had really put in those exclamation marks, or if the editor did it. Mrs. Ramer says not to use them very much.

The interviewer's high voice reached me. ". . . and I understand you have said you are the universe. That's an interesting statement. Very self-confident, one would think."

Daniel sighed. "Not 'I' as just me."

"How's that?" Interviewer out of his depth.

"I mean we all are. You are. The universe is us." Daniel was sounding as if his patience was sorely tried.

Interviewer tries a palsy laugh. "Kind of like 'We have met the enemy and it is us.' "

"I don't think so," Daniel said wearily.

Interviewer gives up. Snaps notebook shut with a smart clap. Dives into brief case. "That's a pretty little cat."

"Thank you." Daniel is being infinitely polite.

"Thank you a lot for your time, Dan. It's been very interesting."

Daniel hates it when strangers call him Dan. A good thing the interviewer didn't say "Danny," or Daniel's politeness might have blown apart.

Interviewer having trouble making an exit. Thanks

Daniel again. Nods to me. Says, "Beautiful old house you have." Pats Lilac, who hisses softly.

From the patio the music drifts in, sounding relaxed, contented, peaceful.

Interviewer gone at last. Daniel comes back from seeing him out. He looks at me.

"Whew," he said.

"Double whew." I put Epictetus back on the shelf.

Daniel said, "Why are so many grownups so dim?"

"Be tolerant," I said, and giggled.

Lilac streaked off toward the patio. Daniel followed.

I dumped the ashtray the interviewer had filled.

Andrew called to me and asked me to pop some corn. Who can eat popcorn after that huge dinner? Andrew, that's who.

I stood a minute looking around the living room, mentally erasing the interviewer from it. Poor guy. Daniel must have really baffled him.

I looked at Mom's favorite chair, and it no longer looked deserted and empty. I thought about the universe being us. It wasn't just Daniel who was the universe, it was all of us. Me. I am the popper of corn, the baker of bread, the writer of stories. I am the daughter, the sister, the friend. I am Katharine. With a plume in my helmet.